THAN THAT

LES ZIG

First published in 2024 by ECG Press
www.ecgpress.com

Copyright © Les Zig 2024

ISBN
Paperback: 978-0-6454853-9-4
Ebook: 978-0-6454853-8-7

Les Zig has asserted his moral rights to be identified as the author of this work.

This book is copyright, and all rights are reserved.

We welcome your support of the author's rights, so please only buy authorized editions.

This is a work of fiction. Names, characters, organizations, dialogue and incidents are either products of the author's imagination or and any resemblance to actual people, living or dead, firms, events or locales is coincidental.

Without the publisher's prior written permission, and without limiting the rights reserved under copyright, none of this book may be scanned, reproduced, stored in, uploaded to or introduced into a retrieval or distribution system, including the internet, or transmitted, copied or made available in any form or by any means (including digital, electronic, mechanical, photocopying, sound or audio recording, and text-to-voice).

This book is sold subject to the condition that it shall not, by way of trade or otherwise, be lent, re-sold, hired out, or otherwise circulated in any form of binding or cover other than that in which it is published and without a similar condition being imposed on the subsequent recipient.

Please send all permission queries to info@ecgpress.com

A Cataloging-in-Publication entry for this book is available from the National Library of Australia.

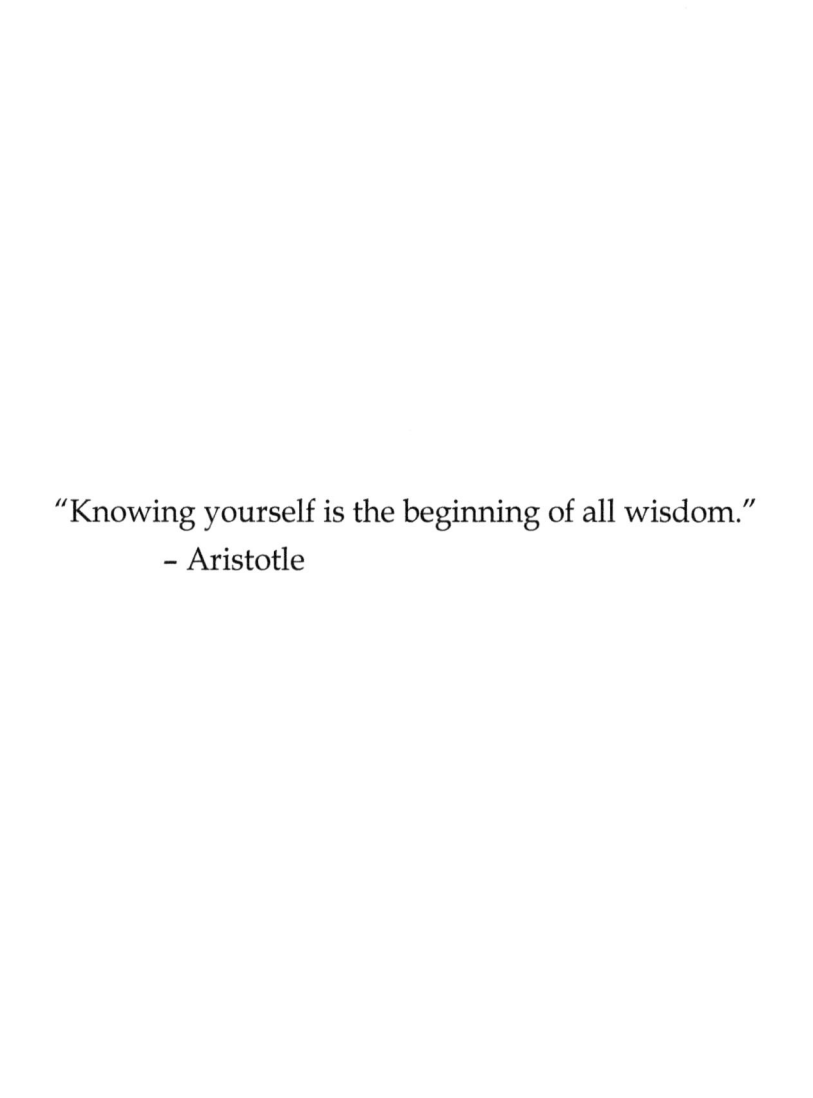

"Knowing yourself is the beginning of all wisdom."
 – Aristotle

1.

Luis waddled toward Sherry, a bloated walrus in a tatty red silk robe, his paunch parting the lapels so his hairy chest, and hairier crotch, were grossly on display. In his right hand, he held a tall glass of vodka.

"We fuck now, yeah?" he asked, his guttural accent lyrical in the way he strung syllables together: *WeeFORKnow, YER?*

Sherry checked her sigh as a wasted breath. Luis was oblivious to social norms, etiquette, and common decency. Creativity had wrestled him into the facsimile of something human, but it was a testament to his talent that his grotesque shtick actually worked with some people. Sherry had heard stories of adoring young editors, publishing interns, and devoted readers he'd bedded.

"No, Luis, we don't fuck," she said. "We never fuck."

"You no go out in rain," he said.

She could hear the savagery of the storm – the pounding rain on the roof, and the branches of the trees scratching the windows, as if they wanted to claw their way in. The house itself might've reeled and groaned, like it was cowering. This was not a night to be out in, but neither was it a night to be marooned here.

"Stay with me," Luis said.

"I've already been here too long. Skip's at home, waiting."

"Ah, Skip. He no mind. He writing."

"Same difference."

"Worth try, yes?"

"No."

It was a running joke, and a stupid one at that, but he was easily amused, and his cachet afforded him his tastelessness and impropriety. The world hadn't changed *that* much, especially given he didn't want anything. He was not only happy being a pig, but an anachronism – his house itself was stylish with its minimalist elegance. It was like he wanted to be the one thing that stood out.

She eased his manuscript – fresh with the army of corrections that had attended his grammar (or lack thereof), misspellings, and occasional narrative meandering – into her faded leather satchel, then tied it snugly.

He plopped into his antique wingback leather chair, vodka sloshing from his glass onto his lap. The chair – the one affectation he indulged – creaked, although whether it was at his weight, or contact with his naked buttocks, was unclear.

"Book good?" he said.

"The book's great," Sherry said.

"You not just say that?"

And here was the only thing greater than his crassness: his insecurity.

"You know I don't say those things." Sherry clutched her satchel to her chest. "But these are the final changes. We're overdue and need to go to layout. Pria wanted this book a week ago. I wish you'd use email—"

"No!" Luis said. "No email. No computers."

Sherry checked her watch - 9.42pm. "There's nothing else, right?"

"I happy."

Luis tilted to his left and emitted a squeaky fart that might've torn a hole in the chair's upholstery. Settling back down, he sipped from his vodka.

"On that note," Sherry said, "I'll be in touch."

Luis planted one hand on the armrest of his chair and started to push himself up. "I see you out—"

"No need!" Sherry headed for the foyer, waving dismissively without looking back.

"You sure?"

"Definitely!" she said, although once she yanked the front door open and saw what confronted her, she almost reconsidered leaving at all.

The night was the sort of night Skip would've written: the remorseless rain, the unforgiving cold, and the merciless wind – these were the clichés Skip enjoyed warping into something unfamiliar, if not subversive, although that wasn't the case now. This was straightforward: it was a shit night to be out.

Skittering across the slick cobbled drive, she fumbled with her Saab's door, and fell into the car. She was already too wet, her navy blazer damp and her hair sticking to her forehead. The car's heating – the stale air hot on her face – offered some comfort, but right now home and a hot bath were the only real salvation.

The storm raged as she took the slow, cautious drive into the city, thunder shaking the Saab while forked lightning fleetingly highlighted buildings that were otherwise stark silhouettes. The streets were just about empty, the headlights of the few other cars splaying in blotchy smears across the windshield. The Saab's wipers squelched almost apologetically.

The dashboard lights gradually dimmed, then extinguished. The headlights flickered off. The Saab slowed, then coasted. Sherry guided the car to the curb and tried the engine. The ignition clicked, but nothing. She tried again. Still nothing. She scanned the dashboard. The tank was full

– she'd filled it yesterday, and an empty tank wouldn't account for the lights going out. It was the battery or the electrical system – neither which she knew anything about.

She grabbed her phone and dialed Skip. The phone rang out to an engaged tone. She started to redial, then saw the NO SERVICE in the corner where the reception should be. Naturally. She tried it again, although she knew it was futile. What else would go wrong?

A landline. That's what she needed, as rare as they were now. She scoured the windows around her – a series of darkened shopfronts, except for one: a single light shone. Tearing off her coat, she wrapped it around the satchel, got out of the car, and charged through the rain.

She was wrong about the shopfront – it was a bar, the façade nothing but paneled glass, the interior old but elegant. The floors were burnished, the ceiling buttressed, the style colonial. Buried under a fanciful arrangement of hanging glasses and bottles was the bar, stools arched around it like sentinels guarding a moat. The square tables and chairs that extended from it might've been a scattering of confetti.

Then she saw the occupant – he had his back to her as he swept the floor, moving with an easy grace that suggested some athletic background.

His faded jeans were tight around his butt, his shoulders broad and rounded; his sandy hair was artfully loose, like he'd just emerged from the surf.

The front door was sunken deep in a dark niche, five steps down, the ornamental light – hanging from the ceiling – off. High up in the door was a round window, a portal broken into four quarters that distorted the interior.

Sherry placed her hand in the face of the door and shoved it.

2.

The door rattling against its lock startled Jake. He clenched his broom handle broom the way he might wield a baseball bat. All he could make out in the door's portal was the top of some dark wet hair.

"The opening's tomorrow!" he said.

"I need a phone!"

Whoever it was must've rocked onto her toes, as her face – unmistakably a woman – poked into view.

"My car's broken down!"

Jake rested his broom against the bar and unlocked the door. The woman brushed past him, a slender figure in a white shirt the rain had made transparent enough to reveal the pink lace of her bra. She had something rectangular wrapped in her coat, which she rested on the bar. Jake closed the door and went into chivalry mode.

"Let me get you a towel," he said. "Phone's just over there – it's a landline."

A door adjacent to the bar opened onto a stairwell that ran up to his second-story loft – little more than a kitchenette, a bathroom-slash-toilet, and a lounge-slash-bedroom overlooking the parking lot. He weaved his way around the punching bag hanging from the ceiling, ignored the damp towels slung over the shower cubicle, grabbed the lone fresh one from the closet, and rushed back downstairs. The woman was just putting the phone down.

"No answer," she said. "Sorry. Nothing else is open and I'm getting no service on my phone."

Jake handed her the towel. As bedraggled as she was, she was stunning – not common with her beauty, nor somebody who appreciated herself through make-up artistry, but a woman with sophistication. But then he made a small revision – she had small, pouting lips that added a hint of sultriness. He liked that, and what it suggested. These were fleeting inferences that might've had no basis in reality, but Jake rated his instincts.

"Thanks," she said, wrapping the towel around her shoulders.

Jake drifted over to the other side of the bar and poured two shots of scotch. He neatly slid one across so it landed right before her hand. She offered a smile, then sipped from it, grimacing; Jake thought she might ditch it, but she downed the rest in a gulp. He gestured to her bundled-up coat with his own glass.

"Got state secrets in there?"

"What?" She frowned. "Oh. Work. Years ago, I left a manuscript in my car, the car was towed, and it became this production to get everything back. Missed a deadline, too. So, I get a little bit paranoid."

She picked up the phone and dialed. Jake topped up her glass. She nodded in acknowledgment.

Jake toasted her.

"You're not open?" she asked.

"I've spent the last six—"

"Damn." She slammed the phone down.

"Who you trying to reach?"

"My husband."

Husband. Not that some dick of a husband mattered, especially one who couldn't come to the rescue of his dainty wife. Jake would've offered her a lift if he had a car. And he would've offered to summon an Uber if he could still afford his own personal phone. A taxi would have to do. He took his card folder from under the register, opened it to the taxis, and slid it across the bar.

"Thank you," she said.

She dialed one of the numbers. Jake sipped from his scotch, then held up the bottle to offer her another – not that she'd drunk much from the second. She waved him off and reported she needed a taxi. Jake fed her the address; she relayed it, thanked the dispatch, and hung up.

"I'm sorry – I should've asked," she said. "Is it okay if I wait here?"

"Sure."

"I interrupted you before – you said you spent the last six ... *what*?"

She'd remembered that had been the last thing he said. Most people would've forgotten or wouldn't have been invested enough to register it. Jake liked that, but it didn't take much. This was just a bonus.

He folded his arms across his chest. She watched him from under long curled lashes.

"I've spent the last six months doing the place over," Jake said, twirling a finger to indicate the bar around him. "Well, me and a friend who's been helping out. Used to be a hole. I'm calling it The Rap."

She arched one brow. "'Rap' with an 'R' or a 'W'?"

It took several seconds for Jake to click that she was spelling it – "Rap" or "Wrap".

"That's my name – my surname: Rappaport." He offered his hand. "The Rap. I'm Jake. Jake Rappaport."

She took his hand. "Sherry Kilian," she said. "Jake."

Jake thrust his chin at her coat. "So, what'd you say was in there – a manuscript?"

"A book; I'm an editor for a publisher – Gray's Publishing. Heard of them?"

"Nope."

Jake could've added he wasn't much of a reader, but that was no way to connect with her. He shouldn't have admitted as much as he had. But he couldn't feign common ground. He used to read before football, casually idling through a book in the change rooms while his teammates went through their own pre-game rituals, but that had been a lifetime ago.

"This is the only copy of one of our author's latest novels," Sherry said. "I was coming back from going over it with him."

"On a night like this?"

"He doesn't care."

"The book any good?"

"It'll be one of those things you'll either love or hate."

Headlights flashed across the window. A horn honked. Taxi had responded too fucking quick.

Sherry gulped down her scotch, then reached into her purse – Jake recognized she was going to scrounge around for money, although he imagined paying for the scotch was secondary. She was going to tip him for his time. That's what women like her did – show magnanimity.

"No, no, it's okay," he said. "My pleasure."

"Are you sure?"

"It's fine."

The horn blared again.

Sherry unfurled the towel and laid it on the bar. Her shirt had dried against her skin and bra. She plucked at the shirt strategically, then picked up her package. Jake hurried around the bar to escort her to the door.

"Thanks for everything – I can't tell you how much I appreciate it," she said.

"You're welcome. If you're interested, our grand opening's tomorrow at 7.00pm – if you're not doing anything."

He swung open the door. The cold blasted them but was no dampener to Jake's amour. She shivered and hugged her package to her chest. He wanted to throw his arms around her and draw her in. The attraction had escalated ridiculously quick – although that wasn't unusual for him – but this one had something, an ineffable quality that intrigued him.

"I'll see," Sherry said. "Bye."

3.

Skip crunched on a couple of Xanax as he grabbed a Singha beer from the fridge. The trip from the kitchen was like an adventure through the world's coldest museum, but these were Sherry's tastes: he strode barefoot down the marble hallway replete with colorful abstracts hanging on the walls, past the pair of Waterford Crystal vases sitting on pedestals to either side of the stairwell, over the furry Afghan rug that tended to slide underfoot, and into his den. Mozart's "Marriage of Figaro" boomed from the stereo, the right speaker emitting a tinny echo that suggested it had a tear.

The laptop cursor blinked steadily at Skip from the emptiness of a blank page. He could almost hear it in tempo with the music, chanting, *Blank page, blank page, blank page* – taunting him like the series of unctuous turds who bullied him through the early years of high school because he'd been an introverted bookish twerp. He sipped from the Singha to wash the sweet taste of Xanax from his mouth.

The screech of the screen door opening drew his attention. Then the front door.

Sherry, bedraggled, charged in, carrying something wrapped in her coat. She dropped it on the leather couch (which she'd picked out for this room) and glared at him. He chuckled – a single syllable: *Heh* – but her sharpening brows told him that was the wrong response. He sprang from his chair, turned the stereo down, and held out his arms.

She didn't come.

"What happened?" he said.

"Car broke down, phone wouldn't work, so I found a landline and called you, but …"

"I'm sorry, I was writing," Skip said, glad his body obstructed the laptop's blank page.

"I had to get a taxi." Sherry sneezed theatrically. "I'm going to soak in the tub." She paused briefly at the door, and threw over her shoulder, "Want to join me?"

This was payback: she knew he didn't want to be interrupted when he was writing, but he hadn't been there for her when she needed him. This was the karmic offering, although he still wasn't sure whether she did this consciously or not. He suspected she didn't.

"I'll be there in a bit," he said.

She left his study and went upstairs.

Skip sank into his recliner, spun twice, then settled before his laptop. He took another Xanax.

The cursor blinked tirelessly. He rested his fingers on the keys. Here it was – the connection: mind, imagination, fingers, keyboard. Now all those disparate streams would synergize. The story would come. The story would come. Skip's fingers weighed heavier on the keyboard. The story. Would. Come.

Nothing.

Nothing.

Less than *nothing*.

Othing.

Skip scanned his novels on the shelf above his desk – three of them, each growing progressively thicker, the design fancier, his name bolder – for encouragement. He could do this. He'd done this before. *He could do this.* Sadly, the encouragement was impotent.

He focused on the laptop screen.

The cursor kept blinking, like a boxer beckoning him in for another round.

He pounded out a paragraph, scowled, deleted it, and started over. Then another, and deleted that, too. As the combination of Xanax and beer calmed

the thoughts whizzing through his head, he tried different approaches – writing about a character, then a setting, then coming at it omnisciently, then abstractedly, opening with a conversation, and on it went, fingers pounding the keyboard harder, faster, but without satisfaction. He checked the time in the bottom right corner of the screen—
11.07.

How long had Sherry been waiting?

The chair was a catapult that fired Skip out the door and stumbling up the stairs as that heavy euphoria that came from mixing sedatives with beer discombobulated him. He crossed the bedroom in several strides but slid to a halt before the open bathroom door.

Sherry lounged in the onyx tub, a pale nymph who might've been ... And that was as far Skip got with his reverence. He couldn't construct anything worthy, anything meaningful, anything *fitting*. Simplicity – that's all he had: her hair drawn back, the bubbly water lapping about her nipples. That was it – a base appreciation. He knelt before her, but heard his imagination unhelpfully tell him he was prostrating himself for her forgiveness.

"Took your time," she said.

"Sorry. The new book – you know ..."

"It must be going well."

Skip leaned in to massage her shoulders. She arched her back, hissed, tightened up, but then slowly relaxed.

"Tomorrow morning, I need to call a tow about the car," Sherry said.

"Where'd you leave it?"

"Just outside the city. Outside a bar. "

"A bar?"

"Some guy refurbishing a bar," Sherry said distantly, as if she was drifting off. "It was the only place open. He let me use his phone."

Skip tensed. "Some guy?"

"Really cute." One of Sherry's eyes opened to peer at him.

"Very funny."

"He *was* cute, though. You meeting Tyson tomorrow?"

Skip frowned. "What's tomorrow?"

"Thursday."

"Am I?"

"Alberto's. Breakfast."

That sounded vaguely familiar. It had to be in his phone calendar, although if it was it was because Sherry had put it there.

"Am I missing anything else?" he asked.

"Your launch Saturday? Book signing Monday at Blaise's."

"At *where?*"

"The bookstore – that's what it's called: Blaise's Bookstore?"

Skip nodded like it was coming back to him. He knew those things were out there, but they whirled around untethered, like kites freed from their strings.

"You need to keep track of this stuff," Sherry said.

"But you're so good at it."

"Skip!"

"Okay, tomorrow, Tyson – I've got it."

It began to seep through – tomorrow was to discuss *Cold Enterprise*, due out Saturday, as well as the new book, which he was meant to turn over to his publisher, Gray's, in a month, but was currently nothing more than an empty document.

"I'll get my car towed to the garage," Sherry said. "You can drive me in, then I'll meet you at Alberto's." She brushed his hands away. "That's enough." She sniffled playfully. "You left me all alone. Aren't you meant to rescue me? Take care of me? Console – "

He kissed her clumsily. She tasted of scotch, which was unusual, because vodka was Luis's drink of choice. Sherry usually knocked one or two back with him to keep his trust; Luis didn't trust anybody who wouldn't drink with him – or anybody who didn't drink, period.

Skip tried to neatly scoop her out of the tub, but between the beer, the Xanax, and his natural inelegance, was uncoordinated enough that he fell in. Water splashed over the floor. Sherry shrieked. Skip played along, as if it had been all part of the seduction. He kissed her again, but his knees slid out from under him, and they butted heads.

Sherry laughed. "Maybe we should take this to bed, huh?" she said.

"Good idea."

4.

Jake tossed in bed, tried to settle on one side, rolled onto his back, then flipped onto his other side.

Nerves. This is what he felt when he ran out onto the field for a game.

He tried running a checklist through his head of what had to be done for the opening tomorrow as a distraction but saw only Sherry. Strange, that she'd enamored him to this extent. He saw her bent over the bar or splayed over one of his tables – tawdry, maybe, but it's how he often saw women he wanted to fuck. That was it: the sex as an outlet. That's how he handled the night before games – the more uninhibited the sex, the better he'd play.

He thought about calling Milo, but Milo would likely be in bed – the cost of a young family – and his few leave passes had to be arranged well in advance. But that was fine. Jake was used to flying solo.

Getting dressed, he called a taxi from the bar's landline, then waited outside. The rain had stopped, but it was cold. He rubbed his hands together.

Within fifteen minutes, he was hurtling up the narrow stairwell into The Back Room. The bar was split into quarters: an elegant lounge, a dance floor headed by a three-piece acoustic band, an array of pool tables, and an open balcony where smokers and vapers would abscond, although now only a few people were huddled out there, shivering.

In the lounge, four elegantly dressed women sat on couches to either side of an oblong marble table. Jake identified their drinks: a Manhattan, a Tom Collins, a Gimlet, and a coke that was probably a scotch and coke. The woman who picked up the Manhattan was most prominent, red hair so bright it was almost orange, skin pale, shoulders and arms supple in a sleek blue dress. She smiled shyly at him, then turned away – so innocent and coquettish. But instinct drove this game. Jake bought two Manhattans from the bar (noting, disapprovingly, the bartender's lackluster form), and approached her.

"Drink?" he asked.

She had a fine scattering of freckles and a youthfulness that suggested she was in her early twenties. Her nipples – possibly an effect of the cold – formed peaks in her dress. Her three friends measured him up; one nodded to Freckles, as if to say, *Have fun*. The other two were more guarded. Freckles shifted on the couch, squashing up against her friend. Jake sat next to her and offered her the drink.

"How'd you know what I was drinking?" Freckles asked.

"It's a gift," Jake said.

"How do I know it's not spiked?"

Jake sipped from it, then offered it back to her.

"Hey, what about us?" one of the wary friends asked, a woman with a square jaw.

Jake half rose, as if he'd buy them drinks. "Sure," he said. "What would you like?"

"We're okay!" The friend who'd given Freckles her approval – a stunner with short hair and a big diamond ring on her third finger – waved away his question.

"You always so bold?" Square Jaw asked.

"Yes."

"Does it always work?" the fourth member of the quartet said. She was a little plump; her dress fit like she was outgrowing it. Jake guessed she'd popped out a kid but refused to accept she'd get her pre-pregnancy figure back. Some women did naturally. Others exercised. This one had no doubt tried, but just wasn't able to.

"Would you rather play games?" he said. "This is the problem with life: we walk around, never saying what we mean. I'd rather do away with the games and just be honest."

"What are you then?" Square Jaw asked. "A poet? Live in your mom's basement maybe?"

Diamond Ring and Miss Plump chuckled, then even clinked their glasses together. They thought they had him worked out. Freckles arched her brows, as if to tell Square Jaw to stop it. Jake didn't mind. He liked the fencing – he'd done so much of it. And outside of him being forward, not one of them had read him.

"A physio," he said. "I specialize in sports injuries."

"You must be good with your hands," Diamond Ring said.

Jake placed his Manhattan on the table, then modeled his hands, knowing it was stupid, but stupid gestures impressed people, and his hands *were* big and his fingers deft as a result of a career in bartending and mixing drinks. Thankfully, his short-lived football career hadn't busted them up.

He patted Freckles' knee – a relatively innocuous gesture that was always a good test of the crowd. Square Jaw's face hardened. Jake picked she was a lesbian which, in itself, wasn't bad, but some lesbians gravitated into man-hating, as if the world should do without them, and *every* advance they made was akin to an assault. She wasn't difficult to catalogue.

Freckles shook once but didn't shove his hand away.

"What do you do?" Jake threw the question out there, but his gaze was fixed on Freckles.

"I'm an accountant for a small real estate chain," she said.

Jake couldn't think of anything more boring, but he questioned her about her job (she'd fallen into it by accident), her dreams (she wanted to get into something or other), and her life (he stopped taking things in at this point), artfully excluding the others until they talked among themselves.

"Want to dance?" he said.

"I shouldn't—"

He dragged her out to the dance floor – she offered an instant of resistance, then let herself be taken with such abandon she might've been weightless behind him. His timing had been methodical – the three-piece began a ballad, and the dance floor lights dimmed. He held Freckles close, feeling her svelte in her hands.

"I'm involved," she said.

"It's just a dance," he said.

She had to know he was lying – pressed against his hip, she had to feel his erection. And he wanted her to feel it, to be flattered by its existence, even if it contextualized the dance as *not* just a dance. But she stayed close – mortified, or flattered, or perhaps a combination of both.

"Where's your partner tonight?" he asked.

"Probably with his friends."

"Probably?"

"We're having our girls' night – I'm not sure what he had planned."

"Things not going well?" he said.

Freckles bit her lower lip – she had the slightest overbite, so the toothiness granted her a youthful awkwardness that was endearing. Jake tightened his embrace, until she rested her cheek on his shoulder. He cupped the back of her head.

"It's okay," he said.

"Sometimes, I feel like he takes me for granted," she said. "We've been together since high school. I know he's going to propose soon, but I don't know if he's doing it because he loves me, or because that's just what comes next."

So, she was an *unloader*, spilling her problems on anybody who'd listen, hoping that somehow, miraculously, they might offer her a solution at best, and validation at worst. Jake had a solution, although it had nothing to do with her partner.

"What're you going to say?" he asked.

"I don't know."

Jake caressed her cheek. "You shouldn't be taken for granted."

"So, what do you suggest?"

"Let's take a walk?"

"I don't know …"

Jake let it sink in – she didn't outright refuse, so she was considering it. "We won't if you don't want to," he said. "But it might be good to get away from the noise, you know?"

He gave her hand the gentlest tug – she leaned into him, and then he guided her from the dance floor and down the stairwell. He kept waiting for her to become deadweight. That would be how she'd decline him. And if she did, that was that – they'd talk, they'd go back up, and he would look elsewhere. But Freckles was needy, and she only clasped his hand tighter. They went out into the cold and slipped into the alley adjacent to The Back Room, nestled in the night, hidden in the shadows, and consoled by ill-intentions.

He kissed her and hiked up her dress, waiting for her to resist. She was tense, like she knew she shouldn't be letting this happen, but her discontentment had encouraged her to emotional needs – more than anything physical, the desire to be wanted. His hand slid into her panties. She bucked back, her butt hitting the wall, but she did not grab his wrist, did not try to extricate his hand.

"This is wrong," she said.

"Then why are you so wet?" he asked.

She was about to protest, so he kissed her, and let her words die in his mouth. Her vulnerability was an aphrodisiac, something malleable that he could wring to his whim. She wanted to trust him – that simple. Some people spent their whole lives trying to find somebody to rescue them. It was probably why she was with the goof she was.

Jake slid a finger inside her – it was for her own good. Her legs, her buttocks, her crotch, all grew taut, but she moaned with some surprise. He gave her one last chance to push her case. When she offered nothing, he took a condom from his pocket, tore open the packet, and fitted it nimbly – he did it with the dexterity of a magician performing sleight of hand. His treatment of her underwear wasn't so delicate – he tore it aside, as if the exertion showcased just how much he wanted her. She was already rising to her tip toes, her right leg coming up; he cradled her buttocks and lifted her effortlessly. She locked her legs around his hips. He entered her and rode her against the wall. She had a desperation that he correlated to Spite Sex – she was doing this because it was a big FUCK YOU to her partner as she embraced something she was sure was absent from their relationship. A few drinks had made that easy for her to rationalize. Tomorrow, the remorse would kick in. That was her problem, though.

When Jake's arms grew tired, he spun her against the wall and entered her from behind; she was pliable in his hands, an artifice that existed for his urges. Her cries sharpened – anybody passing would hear her, but then she went rigid, gasped, and slumped. She knelt dutifully to finish him off. Hands tightening in her hair, he came in her mouth, like he wanted to brand her. She swallowed him, shaking. He eased her to a standing position, applying the gentleness now, fixing her bodice, and smoothing the hem of her dress.

"Bobby doesn't fuck me like that," she said breathlessly. "He fucks like we've been married twenty years."

"Is that what you want?"

"No." Freckles kissed the side of his mouth – the sort of kiss when saying goodbye to somebody. "You know, I never got your name."

"Jimmy," he said.

5.

Like so many things, sex was better in fiction. Skip could make his characters as skilled as he wanted – something he'd never enjoyed in real life given his limited experiences. Characters could be confident. Adventurous. Dominant. They could twist the theory of lovemaking into exquisite practice. Partners would quiver. Explode in ecstasy. Become powerless when overcome in the throes of passion. Fiction was good was like that – reality, not so much.

As he kissed Sherry's neck, he tried to focus on her response, on the pleasure behind her expression (surely not faked), the beauty of her supple body before him, on the softness and warmth and pallor of her skin, but all he could think about was that blinking cursor on the blank page. *I'm waiting,* it told him smugly. His half-hearted erection began losing its rigidity.

Now it was a vicious cycle: since he wasn't hard enough to enter her, he put pressure on himself to be hard, but the only thing he accomplished was recognition of an increasingly continuing deflation, until his cock felt limp and pathetic and tiny between his legs.

He flipped onto his back and sighed.

Sherry curled into him and tangled her fingers in his chest hair. "What's wrong?"

The blinking cursor was a metronome that kept the tempo of his frustration.

"Talk to me."

The failures mounted in his head: the failure to rescue Sherry when her car had broken down, the failure to write anything, the failure to join Sherry in the tub when she'd requested, the failure to make love to her, and now the failure to explain himself to her. She knew he was fallible, but not *how* fallible, that he could be so fallible that he was dysfunctional. Some things were best kept unadvertised, although if she didn't know all this by now, surely she suspected.

"You're still thinking about your story, aren't you?"

She saw only the outcome of his endeavors. That's what had attracted her to him – his brilliance as a writer (or so readers told him he was brilliant). Nobody understood how hard it was to commit a single word to the page. Or the crippling doubt that it would be the right word. Or that it would lead to anything that made sense. Writing was an incremental progression in self-doubt and insecurity with a trapdoor under every step.

"Skip?"

"Yeah," he said, because that was the only thing he could say.

"Can I help?"

"I … well … you know … I think …"

He shut himself up. When writing worked, it flowed eloquently. This was something else he'd rarely experienced in real life – not unless he'd rehearsed it in his head, like his book-launch speeches. It made him think that everything was a fiction, and the only genuine truth in his life was his inadequacy.

Although she said nothing, he could *feel* Sherry waiting. But eventually, she gave up, and rolled onto her back. Soon, her breathing grew deep and steady – she'd fallen asleep. What he experienced was relief that he'd escaped – not her scrutiny, but admission of his own vulnerabilities. It was enough comfort that he soon fell into his own fitful sleep.

Waking the next morning with the bed empty was a portent, even though Sherry was always up and about – and had usually had breakfast – before he woke. But now he ran his hand over where she'd lay; the sheet was cool and smooth and that side of the bed was wholly unoccupied. He tried to shake that meant something more than her getting up early.

Once he'd showered, he rifled through the array of black blazers, pants, and boots with silver buckles in the closet with an increasing sense of disenfranchisement. Here was yet another fiction – the image he'd built, refined, and mastered. The clothes might've been a superhero's costume he donned to fight crime – or, in his case, to aggrandize himself in public.

He's so cool, he could imagine people saying. *So mysterious.* But these weren't even attempts to represent the way people might've actually thought of him. It was a romantic conceit that he recognized as folly but entertained anyway because it gave him some semblance of security.

Sherry was in the kitchen, washing up after breakfast. She was somebody words had never been able to do justice. He could capture her simply: the slacks and blazer with the big lapels that belonged on a Parisian runaway; the wealth of wavy auburn hair she'd bound; the thick, arched lashes she'd cultivated. But these were just *things*. In truth, she was too big for him, or this life, or her job as an editor; she belonged in some Elizabethan tragedy where she could be revered and immortalized, where nobles could court her, woo her, and vie for her favor.

"That how you're going?" she asked.

Skip modeled himself, sashaying back and forth. "Not good?"

She straightened his shirt, fixed his blazer's collar, and redid his ponytail.

"You belong in a 1980s boy band," she said.

"I'll take that as a compliment."

"You shouldn't."

On the drive into the city, a familiar weight built in his chest – that dread that he wanted this to be over and done with. Excursions like this were always time-consuming and he'd much rather be writing – or at least trying to.

He dropped Sherry off at the garage – too preoccupied to kiss her goodbye, instead offering only a half-hearted, "Later", and then drove to Alberto's and parked in their lot.

Tyson was already waiting out front – a big rectangle slab of a man, he was easy to spot in one of his shiny suits, his iron-gray hair molded to his head, his smile white and almost fluorescent, his complexion an exemplar of the solarium that had regurgitated him. He held a book-sized package in brown wrapping.

"Shall we go in?" he asked.

Alberto's was an array of tables spread across a cobbled courtyard, interspersed with palms, and an open kitchen that allowed everybody to watch what was being made. A bar opposite them paraded bartenders who juggled cocktail shakers to the delight of patrons, although at this time of the morning all they were working on was smoothies.

A waiter showed Skip and Tyson to a table and left them with two menus, after which Tyson immediately presented his package, then spun it in his hands, removing a wrapping with each rotation, until he revealed the new novel. The cover was icy blue, a tattered heart melted into a snowy hill. Above it, Skip's name was embossed in gold, and down the bottom was the title "Cold Enterprise". This moment once held reverence. Skip no longer knew what it contained now.

"What else you got for me?" he asked.

"Is that your entire reaction?"

"I *did* write the thing. So …?"

Tyson rolled his eyes, then took a full bottle of Xanax from his pocket and plonked it on the table with a sense of martyrdom. Skip went to take them, but Tyson held them firm.

"You need to get on top of this," he said.

Skip snatched the bottle from him, opened it, and shook a single white pill onto his hand. "These pills helped me write three books." He dry-swallowed the pill.

"What does that tell you?"

"I got on to them too late."

"Or maybe you're capable anyway."

Skip snorted and took another pill – not that he needed this one. It was more to shut Tyson up. Skip had written his first book when he was nobody. It'd sold well – *unexpectedly* well. The pressure to follow up and top sales had crippled his imagination. The pills had helped him get into a mindset so that he could produce – well, until now.

"I know what I'm doing," he said.

"Skip—"

"You want a book? I need them!"

His raised voice drew glances from the patrons at nearby tables.

Skip took a deep breath. "I have it under control," he said.

"What's wrong? Is there something you want to talk about?"

Skip pursed his lips, then drummed his fingers across the cover of his book. "Nope," he said. "Everything's fine." He signaled to the waiter. "Singha beer, thanks!"

6.

Once Sherry left the mechanic's, she started down the street and called Pria at Gray's. Pria answered after two rings in that clear but melodic tone of hers – like an actress who might've played the same theatre role for so long that now the lines not only came naturally to her, but also with an air of indifference that bordered on condescension.

"My God, dear," Pria said, once Sherry had finished her account, "it sounds positively romantic: a stormy night, a damsel in distress, an unexpected hero."

"Not quite," Sherry said, as she recalled Jake standing before her. He'd been somebody who no doubt prided himself on how he looked. And primal. Definitely primal. She'd been able to smell the testosterone – he'd been so obvious. Unlike Skip, whose mind was lost in a cryptic prism.

"Sherry?" Pria said. "Do I still have you there?"

"Sorry – I had planned to come in and drop off Luis's manuscript. I know we're in a rush—"

"It's fine. Take a day or two."

"Are you sure?"

"Of course, dear."

Gold light flashed from a shopfront window. Sherry stopped, and sorted through model ships, books on sailing, scuba gear, and there, as the pride of the display, was a huge golden bell. She saw it hanging in a bar, a bartender ringing it to call last drinks, his bicep flexing attractively.

"Privately, we allow for more time with Luis," Pria was saying. "Not that we tell him, of course. We know he loves his last-minute changes."

"Thanks," Sherry said. "Hopefully tomorrow or the day after."

"I look forward to seeing it – and you."

"You, too."

Sherry hung up and felt a separation of self, as if her physical body opened the door to the shop – a Maritime Depot – while the rest of her remained a step behind. She haggled for the bell more out of a need to negotiate and find compromise, and then caught a taxi to The Rap, when what she should've been doing was going in the other direction to Alberto's.

Through the window she saw Jake stacking glasses into the racks that hung above the bar. His t-shirt molded to his body, his torn, faded jeans snug around his buttocks. He was casual, *relaxed*, although she suspected he'd cultivated that down to an artform. Somebody else was also there, this guy shorter, stockier, wearing a hat with the rim folded up.

Carrying the box that contained the bell in both hands, Sherry nudged open the door with her hip. Jake and the other guy spun to greet her. Jake's eyes widened, a momentary loss of his composure, but even that added a layer to his appeal – an instant of vulnerability. Then he smiled back. He would've been the cool kid in school who dazzled everybody with that smile – teachers he needed to mollify when he didn't hand in homework, friends he'd twist to his whim, and girls he wanted to fuck.

Sherry set the box on top of the bar. "Am I disturbing you?" she said.

"We were finishing setting up." Jake pointed at the other guy. "Milo. Sherry."

Milo had a little mustache that was comically wrong, like he might've been parodying Hitler. His face was affable, caught in an expression of befuddlement, although when he smiled it grew endearing – the ever-reliable affable friend. Every hotshot had one.

"Hi," he said.

Sherry shook his hand. "Pleased to meet you." She turned back to Jake. "I know you said you didn't want anything for helping me last night, but I couldn't leave it at that." She tapped the box. "For you."

Jake opened the flaps of the box, peered in, then eased the bell out. Sherry watched his face, wanting to study every change: first, it was the mystification. Then, as he weighed the bell in his hands, appreciation followed – not for the bell itself, but like he could see the expense behind it.

"I thought it might come in handy around here," Sherry said. "You know, signal happy hour, closing, whatever."

Jake tilted his head, no doubt visualizing the possibilities. It was nice to see him work at a standard pace – unlike Skip, who would've considered the merits of the gift, what alternative uses it might have, and what he might have to get her in return.

"I can't take this," Jake said. "I bet this cost … *lots*."

"It's impolite to refuse a gift."

"Well … thanks."

Jake was so adolescent and awkward then, like a child who'd become overwhelmed because his parents had brought home a puppy. It was a strange juxtaposition; he was breezy, confident, and predatory – definitely predatory – but here was an insight to some area of sensitivity he would usually mask.

He lowered the bell back into the box and went around to the other side of the bar, grabbing some glasses from the rack. "How about something to drink?"

"I need to get going." Sherry walked back to the door. "I just wanted to drop in and say thanks again."

"Hey!" Jake said.

Sherry spun in the doorway.

"You coming to my grand opening tonight?"

Sherry frowned. "I'll see," she said, and although when he'd brought up the opening the previous night she'd had no intention of going, now there was a glimmer – maybe. Why not? It might be something to get out, to unwind, to be with other people.

Then she was out the door.

7.

They spoke meaninglessly over breakfast: Skip talked about how he thought he was gaining weight, how he'd been entertaining the notion of getting a dog (but Sherry would disapprove), and about Sherry's adventure last night (and Skip felt an instant of unease, which he struggled to understand, and reconcile). Tyson – one of the world's great nodders – nodded in all the right places to prove he was in tune with the conversation, but he was quick to finish his omelet, and impatient for Skip to do the same with his French Toast. Once they pushed their plates out of the way, it signaled an end to the informalities.

"How's the new book coming?" Tyson asked.

Skip straightened in his chair, distressed how much his belly poked above the waistline of his pants. "Good."

"You're not just saying that?"

"I'd complain if it weren't."

Tyson nodded again, but the nodding turned into a slow shaking of his head. "That's what you'd tell me to think it was coming along well."

"Life's tough."

"Will you make the deadline?"

"I always do, don't I?"

"It doesn't mean I get any less apprehensive."

Skip clasped his hands in his lap.

"You okay?" Tyson asked.

"I would've liked a break after *Cold Enterprise*."

"Skip, *Cold Enterprise* is the first book in the new big, big three-book contract. Did I mention it was big? *Big!* You're upper midlist and trending. Top of the list comes next. This is the time to consolidate your standing in the literary world." Tyson tried to contain a smile, obviously pleased with some bit of information only he was privy to. "And beyond," he added almost shyly.

"Beyond?"

Tyson leaned in over the table. "I wasn't going to tell you this yet, but there's a chance *Cold Enterprise* could get optioned."

"To become a film?"

"No, a monkey. Yes, a film! A big, big film! I've been shopping it around. *Cold Enterprise* is getting brilliant advance reviews. But this gets even better."

The sudden tightness solidified from Skip's chest to his shoulders and up to his neck. Tyson's enthusiasm was encouraging, but it also brought with it commensurate expectation – and pressure. Pressure asphyxiated creativity – it's the reason he'd started on the Xanax. He was apprehensive about what came next.

"If it gets optioned," Tyson went on, "you'll get first crack at it. That's why we need to keep you burning."

"What do I know about writing a screenplay?"

"What do screenwriters know? Download a few screenplays from the net, see how they're done. Better yet, get some of that software that does all the formatting for you. Then stick in the words."

"Stick in the words?"

"It's not an insult. That's what you do – find the right words to do the right job to tell the right story. You're a word-sticker."

"A word-sticker?"

"Skip, let's not get pedantic. You know what I mean."

"Consider these words I'm sticking before you: I mightn't want to write it."

Tyson had been in the process of lifting his latte to his mouth. He froze mid-motion. Skip knew he wouldn't be able to explain the countless sleepless nights trying to wrangle *Cold Enterprise*'s structure together in his mind, the anarchic jumble interweaving plots, the anxiety of breathing life into one-dimensional characters – Tyson was only interested in the result. Most people were.

"This doesn't have anything to do with artistic integrity, does it?" he asked. "With not wanting to sell out?"

"I'll sell out when the times comes, but I'm done with *Cold Enterprise*. It's out of my system. I've exorcised it."

"Exercised ..." Tyson frowned. "Or *exorcised*? Like an exorcism?"

"Stories are demons. The only way to get them out is an excruciating exorcism. Once they're gone, that's it. Why would you want to swallow it again? You're free. Let this thing go wreak havoc out in the world. That's why you put it out there."

"Skip, we could get you a six-figure salary."

Skip drummed his fingers on the tabletop. He didn't write for the money – that was a bonus. Now it could be a *huge* bonus. This could set him up for life. But now it would be selling out – doing something exclusively for money. Here was more pressure.

"Let me think about it," he said.

Tyson bounced to his feet so urgently Skip thought that he must've needed to dash to the toilet but, no, it was Sherry arriving, and he was being courteous. Each feathered the other with a kiss on the cheek that made no contact, and while they were smiling, each were rigid with wariness, as if preparing to defend themselves.

"Tyson, you're looking well," Sherry said.

"How's Gray's?" Tyson asked. "You're working on Luis's new book? How's that going?"

"It's brilliant – you know Luis is eccentric, but these authors …"

"Oh, thanks," Skip said.

Sherry tousled his hair, then scowled at the Singha. "Already?"

"It's a breakfast aperitif."

"Right." Sherry picked up the copy of *Cold Enterprise*. She flicked through it with indifference – she was never interested in the final product. "Book looks great."

"You're still the best editor Skip's ever had."

Silence as the double entendre hung there. Skip almost cringed. Tyson and Sherry had been going out together when she'd been assigned to edit Skip's first book. A relationship had developed. Tyson had struggled to reconcile the break-up. Now he held out his hands, as if to say, *Oops*. But for as clueless as Tyson portrayed himself, he was sharp. He said nothing by accident.

"Ready to go?" Sherry said.

Skip rose.

"Think about it, Skip," Tyson said.

"I will."

"A pleasure, as always, Tyson," Sherry said.

"And don't forget, Skip, on Saturday—"

"Yeah, yeah," Skip said. "Launch on Saturday. Book-signing Monday at Blaise's Bookstore."

Tyson laughed with such genuine delight, he sounded bizarrely adolescent. "You remembered!"

"Come on, Tyson," Skip said, with a glance at Sherry. "Like I'd forget."

8.

Jake's body solidified into one rigid muscle on the drive up to Hidden Vale. It started with a cramp in his neck. Then his shoulders stiffened. His chest constricted next, and with that came shallow breathing. It would've been easy to suspect a heart attack, or to ponder some greater threat, but he knew this journey too well.

The palatial houses with the spacious yards blurred past. The designation of suburbia was lacking here in Hidden Vale. It was splendor neatly partitioned into each individual resident proclaiming their opulence and magnificence.

Once Jake had turned into Ward Street, the sweat broke out on his brow and his heartbeat accelerated. Although the limit was sixty, his foot was light on the accelerator, while the engine of Milo's VW wheezed with encouragement that he should get a move on.

Jake pulled into the winding drive of Mom's house, parked the VW by her crimson Beamer, and rang the bell. He hoped she wouldn't answer (although they'd arranged lunch, but until she answered there existed the hope she wouldn't), and then he could beg off and tell her he'd made the effort, but the door opened and there she stood in a navy dress, auburn hair tied back stringently, strands of gray glittering. She was still an attractive woman, prim and authoritarian just like she had been in her career as a school teacher (and, later, a headmistress at a private school). Jake had wondered how the students – particularly the boys – perceived her, if they'd gained the same sense of foreboding that he had all his life. A sly aside began – Jake had fantasized about some of his high school teachers. He started to wonder if Mom's students … and then, repressing a shudder, he shut that down quick.

"You're late," she said.

"Traffic," Jake said.

He hugged her, or at least shaped his arms around her lithe figure, and made a sound like he kissed her, although his lips never touched her cheek – Mom's fault, as she lifted her face away from him, almost in trepidation. That wasn't unusual. He might've disturbed the artistry of her make-up although now, instead of stealing years from her face, it succeeded only in painting a caricature.

Jake followed her across a floor so polished it seemed wrong to set foot on it, and past gorgeous landscapes hanging on the walls, as well as curios and knickknacks – vases, sculptures, and abstract pieces Jake still failed to identify – that had been arranged to contribute to some mystical feng shui espousing beauty, harmony, and perfection, instead of what it all amounted to: conceit.

In the kitchen, Mom labored over the oven, preparing a thick pumpkin soup. Unbidden, Jake assumed the duties of cutting the salad and slicing bread from a fresh spelt roll. They worked wordlessly, and then ate wordlessly, seated at opposite ends of the marble kitchen table, Mom sipping from a glass of red, while Jake – as much as he would've liked a beer (Mom didn't have any, and hitting spirits reminded her too much of Dad) – stuck with a glass of water.

"Well," Jake said, once he'd finished his soup.

He pushed his bowl to the middle of the table, then cursed himself. Before he'd even begun to rise from his chair, Mom swept up his bowl, piled it on her unfinished bowl, and took them to the sink. She washed the first bowl, then held it aloft, as if unsure what to do with it. Jake picked up a towel, ready to dry it. She planted the bowl in the dish rack.

"They'll dry naturally," she said.

"You used to make me dry dishes all the time."

"That was about building character, *and* teaching you responsibility – something you've often struggled with."

"Mom, I run a business now—"

"It's opening tonight?"

Jake straightened. "Yeah."

"Jake, is this really the endeavor for you?"

"We've had this conversation."

"We need to talk about this, Jake. Running a business requires maturity—"

"I'm mature!"

"You don't sound mature, shrieking at me like that." Mom deposited the second bowl onto the dish rack, then grabbed the pot from the stove.

Jake ground his teeth.

"You should take a lesson from your father, Jake."

"Mom, Dad's dead."

"Forty-eight. And a heart attack. All his life, doctors told him he had to learn to unwind, to relax, to de-stress. About all he did was drink *more*. He'd never talk. He'd kept it pent up. And drink. Drink, drink, drunk. You are very much your father's son."

Jake shoved his hand in his pocket and fingered the key for the VW.

"Do you really need the pressures of a business and all that debt? Remember how it crushed your father? You could've at least let me help out—"

"Mom, are you coming to the opening tonight?"

"I don't think I should be driving at night. My eyes, Jake. You understand. And it's a young person's thing. I'm sure it will be a party, and I'm not so robust anymore." Mom lay the pot on the dish rack, then grabbed the cutting board. "And you know I'm not one for parties, Jake. Never have been. You get that from your father. I'll see your little club another time."

"It's a bar, Mom."

"Same difference."

Jake slowly drew the VW key out of his pocket, protruding from between two fingers of his clenched fist, the ridges cutting into his palm.

"But I do wish you the best," Mom said.

"I should be going." Jake forced a kiss onto her temple before she could pull away. Her make-up had grown sticky in the heat of the kitchen. He felt its residue on his lips, like she'd marked him to highlight his inadequacies. "Thanks for lunch."

"Of course, Jake. You're my son."

It wasn't until he'd left Hidden Vale behind, speeding down a long stretch of road where the skeletal frameworks of houses were just going up, that he grew light-headed. He veered the car off to the side of the road, clamped the steering wheel, and took deep breaths.

A beer or two would be good, although that would be imprudent before the launch. Sex would be better. Sex would be *much* better. He could fuck this right out of his system. He should've gotten Freckles' number, although he'd left her with a fake name and the unspoken agreement it was a one-off.

Putting the VW back into DRIVE, he hit the accelerator, and pulled back out onto the road.

9.

Sherry perched on the plush leather couch in Skip's den, legs folded under her, as she went through the final corrections for Luis's book. Skip sat at his keyboard, typing spasmodically – there'd be flurries of activity, pauses, heavy keystrokes (Sherry recognized Skip selecting text and then deleting it), and then it would start all over. Twice, he paused to take those stupid pills. It wasn't going well, regardless of what he told her.

"Hey—?" she began.

Skip spun in his chair before the word was even out, obviously grateful to be interrupted, but responding with indignation – throwing his head back jauntily and sighing heavily – as if she'd disrupted some great inspiration, but it was a misnomer. When Skip was writing, *truly* writing, there was no melodrama. This was his imagination coming out in all the wrong ways.

"What did Tyson want you to think about?" she asked.

Skip almost swiveled back to his laptop. "There's a chance *Cold Enterprise* could be optioned. Tyson wants me to have a go at writing the script."

"That's great."

Now Skip did spin a full revolution in his chair. "You think?"

"Of course it is. Book and film are so intertwined nowadays. When do you start?"

Skip drummed the armrests of his chair. "You know I don't like rehashing stuff when I'm done." He twirled back around.

"This is something major, Skip."

"So?"

"You should be excited."

"Meh."

Sherry took a moment to clamp down on her irritation, but then decided this was a situation where Skip didn't need to be coddled. "When did you become so stodgy?" she asked.

Skip stopped abruptly. "Stodgy?"

"Dreary. Humdrum. Pedestrian. Dull. You used to be adventurous."

"Was I?"

"Weren't you?"

"I was manic."

"Then get manic about this."

"I already spent my manic energy on *Cold Enterprise*."

"So, you're not even going to try?"

"I'm thinking about it, but it's not looking good."

Skip idled back around to his laptop; his typing resumed that spasmodic rhythm. It was a clumsy opera. Skip *was* neurotic. He'd been nervous when they'd first had sex and prematurely ejaculated; he'd suffered shortness of breath at functions and was uneasy in public. Several times, he'd had panic attacks. That's why he relied on the pills and the beer.

But he could also compartmentalize his anxiety as a motivator – especially creatively. He could easily channel his energy into an adaptation if he really tried. This, though, was just one of those Skip things – a refusal that he found a way to irrationally justify.

She looked at the back of Skip's head, the tangled but thinning longish hair; watched as he typed to maintain the pretense he was writing; thought about how he'd snubbed her twice last night; and for what? He was a selfish man. He always had been. But his brilliance eclipsed it – or at least enamored admirers to endure it.

Of course, they didn't have to live with it.

Sherry was startled as the nub of her pencil – indenting the page until it had almost poked a hole through it – broke. The exasperation wasn't new. But it *was* growing. She could deal with Skip's quirks as long as he wasn't being wholly selfish, but that's what he was becoming. Or maybe he always had been, and she was just noticing it more.

She took her phone from her pocket, rested it on the armrest of the couch, and sent herself a message. The phone vibrated immediately. Skip sighed, as if it was a monumental distraction. Sherry picked up the phone and held it as if she were reading a text.

"Luis," Sherry said. "Last-minute issues with the book."

"That's Luis."

"I'm taking your car."

"Sure."

Sherry slowly crossed the study, her heartbeat accelerating, her legs growing heavy, her cheeks flushing with warmth. A moment's doubt snuck in as she kissed the top of Skip's head. She shouldn't be doing this. Then she caught a glimpse of the words on his laptop – an incomprehensible paragraph describing a romantic dinner, with the last words comprised of, "Wkjrwkjrkjfkefksjfdjf ldwjfkdljfsdlkjf" and then "fuckfuckfuck".

"I'll see you later," she said.

"Have fun," Skip said.

She left the study.

10.

When Jake got back to his loft, he showered, found the freshest pair of jeans from the mess strewn across the floor, put on a new t-shirt he'd bought just for the launch, and then went downstairs. He relished The Rap's emptiness, its cleanliness, and its quiet one last time.

One of the full-time barmaids he'd hired, Karen, was the first to arrive – she was a buxom blonde who liked her black slacks tight around the hips. During the interview, she'd told Jake she wanted to model, although she was getting on, and had the CV of a career bartender who hadn't realized this was going to be her lot in life. Luke, one of the part-timers, arrived next – solid, unassuming, wearing a pair of rectangular glasses that were a generation out of style, he *was* a career bartender who wanted to pick up a few extra shifts because he and his girlfriend had just bought a house. Then it was Milo, wearing the latest in a succession of goofy hats he'd adopted since high school, taking a stool, and pompously tapping his fingers on the bar.

"Barkeep!" he said. "What do you recommend?"

"Very funny."

"Alice sends her apologies – kids, you know?"

Jake poured two scotches and slid one across to Milo. "To opening night."

Milo toasted him. "To opening night."

"Hopefully, they come."

They did, trickling in at first: friends he'd met working in bars over the last ten years who congratulated him and marveled at the place; acquaintances (and he'd made so many) who were hounds for a night out; and former colleagues, who assessed the place with a professional eye, before nodding their approval. It wasn't long before The Rap was brimming, Karen and Luke frantic at the demand, until Milo had to slip behind the bar to help.

When Sherry showed up, it was minus fanfare. Jake had just poured four beers for a shaggy-haired twenty-something when she squeezed in among the other patrons vying for service. He absently handed over change and ignored people who'd been in the line so that he could greet her.

"You made it," he said.

Sherry held out her hands, as if to say, *Here I am.*

"What can I get you?"

"How good a bartender are you?"

"I'm okay."

"How okay?"

Jake held his hands out. "Hit me."

"Let's start with something simple: a Tequila Sunrise."

"One Tequila Sunrise coming up."

It was an easy cocktail – crushed ice, half a cup of tequila, two cups of orange juice, and then a dash of grenadine, which sank in and provided the red sunset, sitting under the orange blaze.

Sherry held it up, studying it as if it was a valuable artwork from which she was trying to divine the artist's meaning. "Nice balance," she said. "Too many bartenders have muddy sunrises." She sipped from it slowly. "Good."

"Good?"

"Okay."

"Okay?"

"Not great. Rubbish really."

He felt an instant of indignation, and tried to find a retort, but when he saw her smile, identified belatedly that she was joking. He wasn't used to subtlety, but decided it was cute – the banter of early courting. And it made her more fuckable. Payback fuckable. He knew how to tease, too.

Sherry lifted the glass with a flourish. "To your bar – congratulations."

As much as Jake wanted to chat, the demand made it impossible. Sherry drifted to the end of the bar, where a brutish guy in a leather jacket immediately offered his stool. Sherry's smile was beatific. Whenever she wanted a drink (next a Gimlet, then a Manhattan, then a Cosmopolitan) Jake was immediately in front of her – too quickly, he had to admit to himself.

She indulged her would-be suitors, listened to their propositions, and then shot them down with aplomb – all but a twenty-something pretty-boy with a mop of blond dreadlocks who wandered over toward the end of the night, daring her wit when others had been smart enough to diplomatically withdraw.

"Buy you a drink?" he asked.

"Then what?" Sherry asked.

"We talk. Get to know each other better." Pretty-boy traced one finger down her arm. "Sounds good, doesn't it?" He signaled to Jake. "Two of whatever the lady's having."

Jake pushed off from where he leaned against the sink.

"Wait a moment," Sherry said. "I've been trying different cocktails."

"Different is good," Pretty-boy said.

"What would you suggest?"

Pretty-boy scanned the rows of spirits and liqueurs, as if that might conjure the right choice. Something simple. That's what Jake would've gone for. A Tom Collins, perhaps. Something too fancy would be ostentatious. Something too similar would show his ignorance.

"How about an Orgasm?" Pretty-boy said.

Sherry's mouth dropped open. "Was that a line?"

"A joke!" Pretty-boy said. "A joke! That's me. I've got a sense of humor. You'll love that about me. Two scotch and cokes."

"That's not a cocktail," Jake said. "It's a mix."

"You're not doing too well," Sherry said.

"Beer?" Pretty-boy asked.

"What am I going to do with you?" Sherry said.

"I think I should …"

"Good idea."

Pretty-boy slipped away.

Sherry directed a gaze at Jake. "How about *you* surprise me?"

He loved the way she looked – regal and pristine, a woman of high character who might never otherwise deign to amuse herself with a bartender if not for their chance meeting. Well, that was the narrative – at least this time around. Truth was Jake didn't have much experience with women of this ilk, so he was drawing on tacky clichés extracted from shitty movies.

"Are you driving?" he asked.

"I am."

"Got your car fixed?"

"Got my husband's."

"So, where's he?"

"Working."

"At this time?"

"He's a writer."

"Anybody I heard of?"

"Skip Lago."

Jake pretended he was trying to place the name. He envisioned an older man, somebody balding with thick glasses, and a growing stomach – a mentor who'd dazzled her when she was young and impressionable. Now she was maturer. He was boring. Their sex life – which had never been good anyway – had dwindled. She was seeing him as antiquated. The luster had faded.

"You know him?" she asked.

"No."

Sherry laughed.

"Didn't you say last night writers are crazy?"

"They are."

"And hubby?"

"More so."

"Yeah?"

"He'd rather live in his head than out here."

Jake didn't see the appeal. If he had a woman like this, a lot of the time would be spent fucking. He pictured sordid positions. Oral. Anal. There would be no limits. These were thoughts that he fleetingly entertained with partners, and then indulged in, but here they persevered into all sorts of scenarios.

Sherry waved her empty glass around. "What about you? This the dream?"

"This is." Jake held his arms out. "You wouldn't believe the sacrifices I've made to get here: bad jobs, bad hours, sleeping in my car – well, before I sold it – no phone, no luxuries, no indulgences, and a big bank debt all led here."

"Has it been worth it?"

"Personally? Yeah. Financially? Give me a year and I'll let you know."

"So, what's next? A franchise?"

"Who knows? Right?"

"Who knows?"

Sherry lifted her glass to her lips, but only now seemed to notice it was empty. She waved it around. "I'm still waiting for my surprise."

"Sure."

Jake dumped the glass in the sink and grabbed a fresh one. He could keep juicing her up with liquor – she'd already had five, so obviously she wanted to let go. He could feel it. That she was here proved it. Things obviously were worse with hubby than she let on. But Jake didn't want an easy victory. And there was something to be said about nobility.

He shoveled ice into a glass, filled it with water, and slid it in front of her. She examined it, then took a sip.

"Ice water," she said. "Original."

"You should pace yourself. Anyway," Jake checked the clock hanging over the bar, "coming up to closing. And you're driving. Right?"

"Right."

"Time to put your gift to use." Jake rang the bell, which he'd hung up behind the bar. The bell's peal cut through the hubbub. "Last drinks!" He grinned at Sherry. "Not a bad gift."

Sherry lifted her glass and toasted him. "You're welcome."

11.

Sherry knew she should excuse herself and go, although she would've been over the limit. A taxi was out of the question. She wouldn't be able to explain to Skip why she'd left his car behind. He'd conjure a whole narrative – his insecurity was good at that. She was meant to be at Luis's anyway, so there was another complication.

People filtered out as the bartenders gathered up glasses. Jake cleared the lines to the keg, while Milo loaded the dishwasher. This would be the best time to leave – while they were busy. She could use the flurry of the exodus to retreat to the car and nap until it was okay to drive.

Milo grabbed his jacket from a rack by the door. "I'll talk to you tomorrow, huh?"

"Thanks," Jake said, stacking glasses into a dishwashing tray. "Couldn't have done any of this without you."

"Any time."

"And thank Alice for sparing you."

"She's a treasure." Milo flashed that ready smile at Sherry. "Nice to see you again."

"You too."

He led out the two bartenders.

The emptiness of the bar gave Sherry's thoughts room to spill out and pronounce how wrong it was being here. But in that was something titillating – just as there had been those early days of dating Skip, even though she'd been tied to Tyson. And, with Tyson, she'd been with Ethan, a junior editor she'd worked with at Token Publishing, before Pria had head-hunted her for Gray's.

Jake butted closed the dishwasher door.

Sherry fished her keys from her pocket. Water gushed into the dishwasher and filled the silence.

"I should get going," she said.

Jake folded his arms across his chest. His shoulders swelled in his t-shirt. Sherry could tell he'd practiced and perfected these poses – seemingly natural but appreciating his best features. And women liked men who worked out. It showed that they took care of themselves – and Jake very obviously took care of himself.

"I should call you a taxi," he said.

"I'm okay."

"That is if you want to go."

"What?"

"Why else would you still be here?"

"You're right – I shouldn't ..."

Sherry hurried for the door, but it wasn't remorse that drove her. He vaulted the bar, and within a couple of strides had reached the door at the same time as her. He placed a hand on it so she couldn't get it open. He was such a big guy – she had never dated athletic men. And his lust was obvious, manifesting in the way he held himself, in the way he looked at her, and even in the heat he exuded. He was a furnace of ill-intentions, so it was no surprise when he kissed her.

Skip's kisses were tentative and exploring – Jake's were an assault. His hands slid down her back and cupped her buttocks. He lifted her so effortlessly that she enjoyed her helplessness – this was a man who could break her. She locked her legs around his hips like she was trying to temper him. He swung her around; she tilted back onto a table, the ceiling lights blaring in her eyes.

There was a desperation in the way he assailed her, like he wanted to possess her, wanted to strip away all her defenses, tear away all her willpower, and subjugate her to his ministrations, and in most cases it might've amounted to little more than some egotistical self-centered lothario overrating his own prowess and thinking hard and fast meant satisfactory, but one simple reality emerged: Jake was good, and there was a calculated premeditation to everything he did.

Skip was sweet in his clumsiness. Tyson had been ridiculously big but unadventurous. Ethan had been naïve. Others had exhausted themselves and left her unfulfilled. But Jake responded to her every whimper, found every avenue to heighten her pleasure, and drew her to an orgasm where her body grew rigid, and she wailed as ecstasy overloaded and she was sure she was fainting and that everything was becoming black, but when she did become cognizant, she found she was panting, head hanging low over the table.

She sat up, wrapped her arms around his neck, and kissed him.

"You have a bedroom?" she asked.

"Of sorts."

He had a messy loft. A punching bag hung from the ceiling. Weights and other barbells were arrayed in one corner. His bed – a fold-out couch by the window – was unmade, the sheets wrinkled like they'd never been washed. Clothes that stank of mold littered the floor. Unwashed cups, plates, and pans were piled in the adjoining kitchenette's sink.

She pushed him onto the bed and took him in her mouth. He quivered as she tightened her lips around him. She was aware every time his body tensed, of every intake of breath, of what he was and wasn't responding to. His size and strength and assuredness meant nothing now. She had learned how to build rapports with authors by discerning their needs, and how to manipulate them to her standards when they were uncooperative or outright stubborn; Jake's physical cues were no different.

Yanking her blouse over her head, and tossing it clear, she asserted her own authorship, controlling him just as he had done to her. He tried to flip her so he could be on top, but she strutted her knees to either side and pinned his hands over her head. They laughed as they kissed. He could've overwhelmed her (and most men would've), but he capitulated, and she mauled him with gusto more than technique, until he shook, and came.

She collapsed on him and kissed him. His hands closed around her back. He had a different feel to any man Sherry had known. Tyson had been needy, but in a pathetic sort of way. Skip was needy – but it was something else with him, like she completed him, but not in a romantic or emotional sense. Jake wanted her like he was trying to use her own gratification to subjugate her to him.

"I should go," she said, although it was the last thing she wanted to do.

"You okay?"

"Yeah. It's late."

She cleaned up as best as she could in the little bathroom, then hunted down her blouse and bra, and slipped them on as she stormed down the stairs. Her jeans were puddled under the table Jake had fucked her on, but there was no sign of her underwear. She pulled the jeans on as Jake watched, standing there unashamedly naked. Then she sat on a chair and put on her shoes. He came to her when she rose and hugged her. They kissed again. He was a great kisser.

"I really have to go," she said.

She broke free and wrestled with the door. Then Jake was behind her, unlocking it. He swung it open.

"Bye," she said.

The cold of the early morning cooled what remained of her amour. A side alley adjacent to the café next door to The Rap led to the big communal parking out back, framed by a procession of restaurants, cafes, and shops. Her car – Skip's 1970 Mustang – was the only one parked here now. A motion-activated light came on as she crossed the lot to the car. She unlocked the car and turned to The Rap. The single second-story rear window was illuminated, highlighting Jake as some improbably sculpted statue framed in the window. He lifted a hand to her.

Sherry waved back.

Then got into the car.

12.

Skip crunched on a couple of Xanax, then pooled his saliva in the back of his throat so he could dry swallow them. He lifted his hands above the keyboard and wiggled his fingers. *This* is when he became a conduit for his imagination, divining connections between characters and plots that he'd never consciously been aware had existed.

Nothing.

The cursor blinked.

He twirled in his chair, tried again, then twirled some more.

This just didn't want to work.

Once he'd grabbed a Singha from the fridge, he idled through his older work, hoping to find a wavelength that could galvanize him. *Enraged* was clunky by his standards today but its rawness drove the plot and connected with disenfranchised twenty-somethings who empathized with the protagonist's dissonance. *Wasteland* showcased a greater command of the prose, although the plotting was scattered, but by now people had grown entranced with the eloquence of his voice. *Effortless, immersive, thought-provoking,* one critic had gushed. *Midday, Midnight, Dawn* was a confluence of everything working: ambitious plotting, engaging prose, and compelling story – or at least that was what everybody had told him.

He opened *Cold Enterprise*, cringing as he expected to find issues that were too late to correct now the book was in print, but then longed for the purpose behind the writing. Still good – or as good as he could get it, which always inevitably came down to *good enough*. He could even see shortcuts he could take, were it a screenplay.

He closed the folder for *Cold Enterprise* and saw a folder for his short stories. He hadn't touched these for years. Opening the folder, he frowned, unsure what he was doing here. A third of the stories had been published in journals – some when he'd just been starting out, while others had been commissioned from him once his name had grown; another third were unpublished, although Skip thought they were sound; and the final third were early drafts or stories that hadn't worked out.

He began to read, expecting they might be embarrassing, but then with encouragement, and finally – as he mowed through beer after beer – with enthusiasm. He could do something here – a collection maybe. He could use that as leverage to buy more time for the novel. When the screen became bleary, Skip printed out the rest of the stories, and read in bed until he drifted off.

He woke around morning, finding the other half of the bed was empty, but the stories he'd printed – some of the paper scrunched up, so he slept on them at some point – piled neatly on his bedside table.

Rolling out of bed, he hit the toilet, and then staggered into the kitchen. Sherry was pristine in jeans and a white shirt, her hair tied back, as she made pancakes. The empty Singha bottles were lined up on the sink like soldiers summoned to revelry.

Skip sank into a kitchen chair. Sherry grabbed the orange juice from the fridge and poured him a glass, then kissed the top of his head – he couldn't remember the last time she'd done that as a morning greeting, but was embarrassed to realize that she might've been doing it all along and he just hadn't registered it.

"Hey, sleepyhead," she said.

Skip gulped down the orange juice; it washed away the foul aftertaste of a night replete with too many beers. Sherry lay a stack of pancakes in front of him, then followed it up with a bottle of maple syrup. Skip's stomach churned.

"What's this?" he asked.

"Something different. You don't eat healthy enough."

"This isn't healthy."

"It is compared to what you'd usually have." Sherry waved at the empty Singha bottles.

"What time did you get in last night?" Skip twirled the maple syrup over the pancakes.

"Late. You know Luis."

"You drink with him?"

"Not much choice with Luis."

"You should watch the drinking."

"Ha. Look who's talking."

Skip shoveled some pancakes into his mouth.

"So …?" Sherry said.

Skip braced himself. The pancakes came with a price.

"What's with the stories you printed out?"

"Oh." Skip resumed eating. "I thought maybe I could do a collection."

"Of short stories?"

Skip nodded. "Thus the word *collection*."

"When's the last time you looked at them?"

"Been a while. Honestly, I have only the vaguest memories of some of them. But there could be something there."

"Something there?"

"Yeah."

"Something *there?*"

"*Yeah.* Why?"

"Yesterday you told me you didn't want to revisit *Cold Enterprise*, but you want to revisit these short stories? Where's the consistency?"

Skip ate more than he should to keep his mouth occupied. He couldn't tell her he thought the collection might work to leverage an extension for the novel, because she didn't know the novel was in trouble. Nobody *could* know, especially with the new contract hanging over him.

And she'd always thought him such a star, a storytelling powerhouse – as much as marriage had pockmarked that affectation, he couldn't shatter what was left of it. He didn't know if he could believe in himself if somebody didn't – at least somebody meaningful like Sherry.

"A collection could be good," he said. "Plenty of authors do them."

"You claim you don't want to go backwards and now you're telling me you want to go backwards."

"What does it matter?" he said.

"I'm struggling to understand your logic."

"What's there to understand?"

"You say one—"

Skip shot to his feet, the chair screeching behind him. "What does it matter?" He dumped the fork onto the half-eaten pancakes. "I write what I'm passionate about. That's all it comes down to. I have no passion for a screenplay adaptation of *Cold Enterprise*. Maybe I will one day. Right now, I don't. I feel something for a collection. I don't know if I'll do anything about it. But at least I feel *something*. And that's all it comes down to. What *I* feel."

Skip knew they were the wrong words the moment he spoke them. Without Sherry, his first novel, *Enraged*, may have only ever been regarded as some crude novelty. She hadn't just improved it but saved it – and launched his career in the process. Her searching, insightful, and always diplomatic editing had challenged him to evolve as a writer. He would be a hack without her, and yet here he was telling her it was all about him.

"Okay," she said. "Fine. What *you* feel."

She left the kitchen. Skip heard the screen door to the back clatter open and shut.

He sank into his chair and poked at the pancakes, tempted to ditch them as a *fuck you*. But the guilt welled up immediately. He ate what remained, although now the pancakes were tasteless, and the maple syrup might as well have been glue. He washed up, commending himself on his magnanimity.

It wasn't until he was back in the study, Mozart's "The Magic Flute" opera blaring at a volume that left no room for any other sound, the blinking cursor on the laptop continuing to mock him, that he pinpointed he wasn't being magnanimous at all.

13.

As he swept up, something bright red under one of the tables caught Jake's attention. Kneeling, he sorted through a mound of rubbish – among other things, fallen coasters, crumpled serviettes, and broken straws – thinking he was going to find a handkerchief or something like that, but the lace that draped over his hand turned out to be Sherry's underwear. He looked up guiltily at Milo, dressed in his greasy coveralls, wiping down a table. Jake scrunched the underwear into his pocket, then continued to sweep until he'd worked his way back to the bar. He brushed the rubbish into a dustpan, then deposited it into a bin.

"That about does it," he said.

Milo finished the last of the tables, bundled up the rag he'd been using, and tossed it to Jake. "Place comes up all right after a big night."

Jake nodded proudly. "She does at that."

He fixed coffees, while Milo sat on a chair, lifted his feet onto one of the tables, and pulled out a battered paperback (a thriller, entitled *A Time to Run*). He splayed it across his lap to a dog-eared page.

"Thanks again for all your help," Jake said.

"My pleasure. So …"

"So?"

"About last night …" Milo said.

"It was a good night, huh?"

"You're being coy." Milo pointed a finger at him. "Why're you being coy? You're never coy. *Never*. You're usually describing everything in lurid detail until I tell you to shut up."

"Really?" Jake brought his coffee over. "I think you're exaggerating."

"Didn't you tell me you picked up some poor vulnerable woman and made love to her in an alley?"

"It wasn't making love—"

"Sorry."

"Thank you."

"You don't make love. You *fuck*."

"Hey, hey, hey—"

"You're the fuck machine."

"A little class - please."

"You gave her a false name!"

"I—"

"That's *your* form, Jake. And you always tell me like it's confession. Now don't bullshit me, okay?"

Confession. Jake was unsure why the word startled him. He'd always thought Milo quizzed him out of that same insecure neediness he'd exhibited at high school, but Jake realized just how ridiculous that was now. Milo was married, a father, and co-owner in the garage where he worked. He was mature. Confident. Sometimes, Jake worried Milo had outgrown him - and their friendship. If his need for details wasn't a need at all, wasn't some vicarious thrill, then maybe this was all a confession, although if that were the case Jake didn't know *what* exactly he was looking for.

"It's nothing," he said.

"Beautiful woman, an obvious attraction, a few too many drinks, and now this coyness," Milo said. "I've gotta give it to you - this is new—"

The Rap's phone rang. Jake sprung over to the bar to answer it like he wanted to springboard out of the conversation. Sighing, Milo flipped his novel and began to read.

"Hello, this is The Rap!" Jake said. "Jake Rappaport speaking."

Silence – or at least an absence of words. Jake pinpointed other sounds: the wind (so the caller was outside), the lapping of water (no doubt a pool – Jake had cleaned pools as a teen to buy his first car, so he knew the sound well), and the soft breath (tentative).

Sherry.

Here it was: the Remorse Call.

"Hello?" he said.

"Hi."

Yep, Sherry. Then silence again. She was probably sitting on a banana lounge in a bikini, or possibly even topless, trying to tan that chalky skin while she reconciled letting loose. Other women buried it. Some found it an avenue to be secretly easy and have a good time on the side. Startlingly few were honest.

"You okay?" he asked.

"Can we talk?"

"Now – ?"

"No, not now. Tonight."

"Tonight, then. You sure you're okay?"

No answer. Not even the wind. She was gone.

Usually, a phone call sufficed – or even a text. But she thought she owed him the decency of doing it in person. She wasn't just a class above anybody Jake had ever fucked, but in another stratosphere. Bizarrely, that appealed to him – somebody who didn't behave like any of the others. It was new. Exciting. And had an allure that he didn't understand outside of it being different. He would've been done with any other woman. He wanted this one again. And again.

He hung up the phone and almost smiled. "Well," he said.

Milo lowered his paperback and frowned. "What?" he said. *"What?"*

14.

Sherry rose from the banana lounge, the weight of guilt so leaden in her chest that it made it hard to breathe. She'd cheated. And as much as she could've blamed the cocktails, a growing dissonance or some other frivolous rationalization, the truth was simpler: she'd gone out, she knew she was attracted to Jake, and while it hadn't been premeditated, she was sure in some part of her mind it had been a possibility.

That invited a whole new stream of thoughts, and something she wasn't ready to face – not Skip per se, but what he now represented: the possibility that this relationship, this marriage, had grown so tenuous that fidelity had become pliable.

Going into the house, she leaned on the jamb of the door to Skip's study, unsure what words were going to emerge. This was what she was meant to be good at – honing language into the weapon that would deliver an irresistible message. But even that was wrong. Everything was wrong.

Skip glared at his laptop, his fingers firing the occasional salvo across the keyboard, followed by pounding BACKSPACE. He slid his hands into his hair. The widow's peaks had crawled higher into his cranium. His hands seemed thin, almost feminine.

Sherry crept up behind him and clasped his shoulders. He stiffened, but she kneaded his muscles until they loosened. She could smell last night's beer on him – or maybe this was how he smelled all the time now. She dug her thumbs deeper into his shoulders like she could wring it out of him, and make him something he wasn't.

"I'm sorry about the argument," Skip said.

"I wish you'd talk to me."

"I have a way of doing things that works for me …"

"I know."

Every good author had their own methodology. Sherry had prided herself on finding a way to connect with each of them. Peculiarly, Skip was hardest of them all. Perhaps that's why she'd confronted him – because his obstinance could be so restrictive. Jake was the opposite. That may've been why she was attracted to him – he was open. Totally. And *upfront*. But he was also *wrong*. Skip was her husband. And she wanted to find an anchor here.

"Let's do something," she said.

"Like …?"

Sherry spun him in his chair and straddled him. She kissed him; he tasted of mint-laden beer – he'd brushed his teeth, but that could do only so much, and in its way it warped the beer into something it shouldn't be.

"Let's get a room in the city," she said. "We'll grab dinner, have a few drinks, and then …?"

Like when he'd been stuck three quarters through the revision of *Midday, Midnight, Dawn*, the deadline looming. The night had ended with them fucking on the coffee table in their room at the Sheraton, then on the twenty-fifth-floor balcony, Sherry braced against the balustrade. That had been one of his better nights sexually – adventurous, although not as long as she might've liked. The next morning, she'd awakened to him sitting cross-legged on the floor, naked, scribbling notes on a series of napkins.

"Can we take a raincheck?" he said.

She pecked him. "Why don't we go away? You can bring your laptop."

His pupils dilated – the prospect horrified him. He was so fixed in habit that anything that might take him away from his writing was deemed wasteful. He hated holidays because they not only meant leaving the comfort of home and his routine, but also came with that implication that while holidaying, he should be doing touristy things and getting away from work entirely.

"Or let's go out tonight," Sherry said. Something smaller. Baby steps were too big for Skip. He needed fetal steps. "Let's go out for dinner."

"I'm really onto something and I don't want to lose it."

Sherry forced a smile. "Okay." She rose and caught a glimpse of the cursor blinking on an empty screen. "I'm going back to Luis's."

"Again?"

"I need to be sure he's done. Pria's hounding me. Have to take your car again – mine will be ready tomorrow morning." She started for the door.

"Hey?"

Sherry turned.

"You okay?"

"Yep."

But anger now fueled every step. It burned not just at Skip, but at the situation: that he could be so ambivalent, that he wouldn't question her feeble alibis, that she could be so weak, and that this whole relationship could putter out, as if it had become so insignificant. The only one innocent in this was Jake: he might be a predator, but he was doing what he knew best.

And as inflexible as Skip was with his quirks and routines, at least Jake was malleable.

Well, as long as he got what he wanted.

Or what he thought he wanted.

15.

When the door clattered open, Jake knew it wasn't Karen arriving for her shift. Karen didn't fling the door open; she was delicate, easing it open just enough to slip through. This was dramatic – a herald to announce an arrival: Sherry, flustered, wide-eyed and so delightfully vulnerable. She might've told her husband. Honesty was the stupid move, but some people needed it.

Jake turned to Milo. "Can you mind the place until Karen gets here?"

Milo nodded. "Go ahead."

Within a minute, Jake sat on the corner of his unmade bed as Sherry paced back and forth. He wanted to strip away her blazer, her blouse, and her slacks – shred the clothes from her like she was a wrapped gift he couldn't wait to open. Her dick of a husband wouldn't take her like that; Jake wanted her in his hands, wanted to feel her lips, her body, to drive into her until he rammed the anxiety from her and only her need for him remained.

"Is your friend working here?" she asked.

"He's just helping out here and there until everything settles," Jake said. "You know, teething jitters."

"Teething jitters?"

Jake nodded. "You didn't come here to talk about Milo. You're upset. Did you tell your husband?"

"No."

That surprised Jake, although he didn't let it show. He decided he liked it – liked that she could be furtive. Slutty. She had that in her. Good. Every woman he'd bedded *did* ultimately.

"I don't want you to think I fuck around," Sherry said.

"So, what if you did?"

Although Jake *was* glad. It would've tarred her as *too* common. He liked that she was his to do with as he pleased, and he sensed she liked that, too – she wanted to be desired, but she needed to be the focus of one man's attention. *His* attention.

He took her hands. Her arms grew rigid.

"Lately I've been feeling a sameness about my life." Sherry's lower lip trembled. "I feel like I'm coming apart, and I don't know what's left of me."

"I get that."

"You do?"

"For years I worked in other people's bars, until I started thinking, *What's in this for me?*"

"That's what I feel at home. I try to make my marriage work, but he's lost in his writing. Nothing else exists to him. I have my own needs."

"What needs?"

A small smile curved her lips. Jake tugged her hands so she came down onto him. He used her momentum to roll with her, so he ended on top of her. Her hands came up, but stopped just before they met his chest. Then she planted them gently, like she didn't want to push him away, but wanted to be in union with what she touched.

"This has to be worth something," she told him.

"What do you want it to be worth?"

"It's not just some fling," Sherry said. "It might not work out, but we'll see? It's about finding something in each other now ..."

Danger signs. *Finding something in each other.* Usually, he would've told the woman the sex had been great (even if it hadn't), but that was all it had been – he was incapable of a relationship, broken, no good for them, and so he would unravel as much as required to paint himself as unpalatable as a long-term prospect. If they had a husband, Jake would feign guilt, imbue it within the woman until she was ready to retreat, and then he'd tell them to go back and make their marriage work. But he wanted to hear Sherry moan and whimper in his ear again and again and *again*, although he wasn't sure why.

He kissed her and slid a hand into her pants. She was already wet, and quivered when he found her clit. He wanted to be inside her, wanted to see her face contort in ecstasy and disbelief, but she scrambled over him, pulled his pants down, and took him in her mouth.

In Jake's history of oral sex, he'd enjoyed, and endured, many different experiences: women who were perfunctory, women who had the subtlety of suction at the dentist, women who bit, women who used their tongue like they were thumb-wrestling his cock, women who kissed and stroked, women who literally blew, women who were so good he could let himself go and relax, and even one woman, a porn star, who'd been so brilliant he'd had the most explosive orgasm ever, but never in all those occasions had he felt so aroused that he might lose it prematurely.

He ushered Sherry up. She blinked at him, his erection perched below her mouth, like the glistening controller of some misbehaving marionette.

"It's not good?"

"It's *too* good," he said.

He forced himself to get moving, at first atypically uncoordinated, but then finding some purpose out of muscle memory as he undressed her and went down on her – more as a delaying tactic to get himself under control than anything. When they fucked, it was a battle of positions, like each could batter the other not only into orgasm, but deference. He usually wouldn't surrender, but found an inexplicable joy at being at her whim.

Jake had the score at one apiece – she'd capitulated to him in the bar, and he'd capitulated the second time around in the bedroom.

He fucked her hard, her calves splayed on his shoulders. Then she was bouncing on top of him, like she was trying to pound him through the mattress. He took her from behind, only for her to command that he fuck her harder and faster. Coming from her, the words weren't profane, but elevated and intoxicating.

There was no union here, but a genuine contest of wills articulated through their bodies. He came first – he couldn't help himself – but he was ready quickly again, and when he brought her to orgasm, face down, trembling beneath him, she wailed so loud he was sure they must've heard her in the bar.

Their respite was brief; they fucked around the loft: over the kitchenette counter, leaning against the window so they could look down into the parking lot, and then finally, and clumsily, in the shower. She locked her legs around his hips, and he fucked her against the wall. Two tiles dislodged and crashed to the floor. It didn't slow Jake. He wanted to explore every possibility in how he could take her, and her willingness was only a challenge to find some resistance he could dominate, conquer, and own.

"I don't know what I'm doing," she said at the end of the night, when he spooned her on his bed.

Jake traced a hand over her hip. "Why do you have to know what you're doing?"

Sherry rolled over to face him. "We're adults. We should know what we're doing."

"Can't something just be?"

"Life isn't that simple."

"Do you like to fuck?"

Sherry frowned, then laughed. "What?"

"Do you like to fuck?"

"I think, yeah – obviously."

"That's as simple as it gets. Like you said, it's finding something in each other now. This is *now*."

Her face grew thoughtful. He loved using a woman's perspective against them.

"Life should never be that complicated," he said. "Or stressful."

"The future always is."

"Who wants to worry about the future?"

"We all have to – sometime."

Sherry sat up. The dishevelment of her hair betrayed her composure. She seemed a pale little thing – at least compared to him; somebody he could wrangle to his own desire, somebody he could bend and stretch and lift to breaking while getting her to scream for more – but at her core, he could feel her resolve and liked that, too. She wasn't weak. Or ditzy. Or trivial.

His erection stirred, but she was already getting up and putting on her clothes.

"I really need to go," she said.

He pulled her to him; she fell onto his lap and laughed. Kissing her neck, he cupped her breasts under her unfastened bra. She squirmed free, nimbly latched her bra and buttoned her shirt.

"I don't know what this is," she said.

"Pretty obvious, isn't it?"

"Beyond the obvious, beyond the now." Sherry leaned over and kissed him on the lips. "Bye."

Jake didn't try to stop her.

She'd come back once.

She'd come back again.

16.

Sherry's deep, rattling breathing – her equivalent to snoring – woke Skip the next morning. He sat up groggily, cold tingling across his shoulders. Sherry slept obliviously, her naked chest heaving rhythmically, her long, wavy hair – so dark now – splashed over her face. With two trembling fingers, Skip eased her hair back. She shifted but didn't wake. Here was a mundane juxtaposition: so beautiful, so sophisticated and classy (or at least he'd always thought), but her snoring was a rusty saw that cut into that image. He kissed the top of her head and eased the covers back up to her chin.

If he'd known in high school that somebody like him could end up with somebody as brilliant and stunning as Sherry, he would've thought that the most improbable fiction of all. But now as she lay before him, she was a disruption in his reality that he couldn't reconcile.

He eased himself out of bed, grabbed a juice from the kitchen, and retreated naked into the study. As his laptop powered up, he popped three Xanax onto his hand – the most he'd ever taken at once. He dry-swallowed them in one gulp. At some point, his imagination had to begin producing. The only alternative was he might have nothing left. Surely it happened to writers.

But, as he poured through his short stories, he grew increasingly excited. There was something here. It didn't have be a stopgap. He recognized the drive and passion that had been missing too long. This was what he had to gravitate to – whatever form the passion took, he had to nurture it.

Hours later, Sherry found him bent over his laptop, squinting – at this rate, he'd need another bout of laser surgery. But he'd earmarked which stories he would use, which were maybes, and which were irredeemable. And while they were irredeemable, conceptually they weren't unsalvageable; they teased ideas for new stories, so maybe the qualification on his block was exclusively on the ideas for his next novel.

"What are you doing?" Sherry said.

Skip leaned back in his chair.

"It's not going well, is it?"

Skip grimaced.

She was striking in a pink dress with shoestring straps and cut low down the back. Her hair was bouffant, and tossed to one side, a dark and brooding scarlet that suggested a tumultuous passion beneath an implacable façade. Her lipstick was a plush red that formed her mouth into a sultry pout.

"Why won't you talk to me about it?" she asked.

"I'll find my way."

"With beer?"

"Hey, I'm not drinking now."

"Xanax?"

"They help—"

"They don't help. They're dangerous."

"I have it under control."

"Mixing drinking and sedatives is dangerous."

"Not in doses—"

Sherry pointed at the laptop. "That's a short story."

Skip considered the possible routes: diplomatic, evasive, and confrontational. He'd messed up their last exchange in the kitchen and had regretted it. Regret was the last thing he needed now – it would just occupy real estate in his mind that his imagination needed.

"Maybe that's the way I need to take," he said.

Sherry bit her lower lip. Skip could hear her objection: *Maybe adapting* Cold Enterprise *to the screen is the way you have to take.* And it was a perfectly fair observation. If she said it, he *would* be magnanimous this time. They could talk about this – well, he could try. He hated talking about anything in development, but he'd find a way. He knew these were all surface-level thoughts, though – cheap and easy. The depths were saved for his writing.

She opened her mouth.

He braced himself, trying to find words that had no meaning.

"Get dressed," she said.

"For?"

"*Your* launch."

"My launch?"

"Today, Skip. *Cold Enterprise* is being launched!"

"Oh, sure. Of course."

"I'm going to pick up my car beforehand and drop Luis's manuscript off at Gray's."

"Okay."

Skip showered, then rifled through his closet. He frowned at the assortment of black blazers, black shirts, black pants, and belts. Black used to be cool, mysterious, and a sign of status, but now all he saw was affectation. Like the Singha, the Thai beer he drank – he'd tried it once, years ago, and had decided that it would be his beer of choice not because he relished its taste above all other beers (although it was a good beer), but because it sounded exotic, and by virtue of that its mystique could rub off on him.

Did he need to keep presenting this face to the world? Did it matter what they thought? He'd made it on ability, rather than presentation. Everything else seemed so redundant – something to impress others. It had become a uniform that had grown ill-fitting.

He settled for a black blazer and collar-less black shirt buttoned halfway up, but a pair of faded jeans – although they'd grown tight around the waist – and a pair of boots. Change should come gradually.

Hurrying down into the kitchen, he expected Sherry would be waiting impatiently, maybe even pacing, but she was staring forlornly out the kitchen window, her arms folded under her chest. When she saw him she smiled almost maternally, like she took some amused pride that he'd chosen his clothes out for himself. She came over and began to button his shirt.

"Not the top one," he said. "You know it makes me feel like I'm choking. God, I hate these things."

"What?" Sherry asked. "Your casual attempts at a suit or book launches?"

"Either. I'm easy."

"Drink your way through it the way you usually do."

"Don't think I'm not going to take that as encouragement."

"Naturally. So, it's going to be another drunken night? Another night I put you to bed?"

"It's a survival thing."

"Don't you think it's time you did a little growing up?"

That was unexpected – and hurt. Skip wondered if it was a lateral sally at his refusal to adapt *Cold Enterprise*. He wasn't doing the mature thing. He remained locked into whim. He always had to have his own way. His mind raced off the possibilities, but before he could muster a response, Sherry ran the fingertips of her left hand down his stubble.

"You couldn't shave?" she asked.

"I did shave."

"Two days ago?"

"You know I time my shaving to get the right level of growth for occasions."

"How about shaving today?"

"Nobody wants to see me smooth-faced. I don't want to see me smooth-faced."

"You're hopeless."

"I try my best."

"You ever considered maybe trying something different?"

"It's who I am."

Sherry took a deep breath – she coddled him when they first got together, encouraging him and assuring him and challenging any of his negative self-perceptions. But that had stopped. Skip couldn't work out if she'd given up, accepted him, or he'd stopped seeking that validation. It was pathetic – he'd been pathetic. Maybe that's what she'd identified.

"Drop me off at the garage and I'll get my car," she said. "I'll drop Luis's manuscript off, then I'll meet you there, okay?"

"No problem," Skip said.

Sherry clasped his hands, then rose on her tiptoes and pecked him on the cheek.

17.

Jake leaned against the bar, wringing his hands nervously as he watched Mom navigate The Rap like she'd been dropped into a labyrinth and wasn't sure what course to take. She ran a finger over a table, then regarded her entire hand as if it had become coated in shit. Jake sighed, letting it out long and slow to spread his frustration. He shoved his left hand in his pocket and fingered the lace of Sherry's underwear. He really needed to put that way. His gaze flitted to the set of drawers under the bar, but just as he was about to reach for them, Mom spun grandly to face him.

"I suppose it's nice enough," she said. "Rustic in its way, isn't it?"

"Can I get you a drink?"

"A drink?"

Jake held his arms out wide. "It's a bar, Mom. People come here to drink. Maybe I can fix you something fancy – a cocktail."

"Jake, it's mid-morning."

"Of course. I'm sorry. Yes, you're right."

"Is that what you do with your mornings? Drink?"

"No—"

"Are you sure?"

"Yes—"

"Then why offer?"

"It's a habit—"

"Your father drank mid-morning. He drank all day."

Dad had been a high-functioning alcoholic, although Mom never acknowledged that. She knew he drank too much, complained he drank too much, but never conceded what that might've meant – that would've been a blight both on her marriage and, more importantly, herself. Problems only existed when they were yanked into the open. But that was a dangerous course. Mom offered only unrelenting condemnation. Jake knew that well enough from experience.

"You do get people in here, don't you? I would hate to think you've put in all these resources—"

"It's been good, Mom."

"Hmmm."

Although the sun bathed the hardwood floors in volcanic gold, Mom stood in the chasm of a shadow – right in front of where the wall between windows blocked the light. She emanated a chill that filled The Rap until Jake could feel the bar recoil, wanting to regurgitate her.

The door opened and Milo traipsed in, again in his greasy coveralls. He stopped at the sight of Mom.

"Oh, hi, Mrs. Rappaport!" Milo started for her, then stopped and held up his greasy hands. "Probably best not to greet you."

"Don't be silly, Milo."

Mom hugged him briefly, and kissed him on the cheek, although Milo kept his hands folded behind his back.

"You're looking well," she said. "What're you doing here? Aren't you working?"

"I thought I'd drop by on my break."

One of Mom's finely plucked eyebrows arched. *And?*

Jake waved his hands back and forth to signal Milo shouldn't explain.

"I've been helping Jake out while he's been ..." Milo finally caught Jake gesticulating.

"While he's been ...?" Mom asked.

"Getting started. Nothing much really. I'm just down the road and stuff."

"I hope Jake hasn't been taking advantage of you. And that he's been paying you. You have your own life, Milo. You have a wife. You have children. Like most men your age. That's what age does, after all. It invites responsibility. Only the mature accept that invitation."

"They understand that it's temp—"

"Don't take them for granted, Milo."

"I wasn't—"

"And you ..." Mom's eyes flared. "When are you going to settle down?"

"Mom!" Jake said.

"We need to talk about this. Living this rootless existence. You should find yourself a nice young woman. Maybe that'll help provide some stability to your life. Working all over the country in seedy bars and strip clubs and brothels."

"Mom ..." Jake said.

He'd worked the bar one night in a brothel as a favor, admitting it as a joke he thought they could all laugh about. Dad had. But Mom had extrapolated a possible future that had involved a descent into drugs and porn that would ensure no self-respecting woman would ever be interested in him, and that was what was important, after all – not the drugs and porn, but landing a self-respecting woman.

"You can be perverse. Do you know that, Jake? Perverse. Like your father. Watching internet pornography nonstop. My Lord!"

Dad had worked tirelessly all day, building a lucrative catering franchise. One time, Mom had found him watching pornography. Just the once. And it wasn't like it was anything deviant or fetish. Jake suspected (but never had the courage to ask, and thus have confirmed) that given it was late at night, Dad was trying to arouse himself in preparation for Mom. His weakness had been his inexplicable devotion to her. Or perhaps it had been his subjugation.

"Take my advice if only once in your life," Mom said. "You need to focus on something greater than yourself."

"I'll try."

"You'll try." Mom checked her watch. "I have some shopping to do. And you'll be opening soon, I imagine."

"We don't open until one."

"Hmmm. A short day."

"Mom, I work until …" Jake gritted his teeth. It was pointless. "Thanks for coming."

"You're my son. Of course I'd come. And it's a nice place. A bit quaint. But they've always been your tastes."

"Yes, Mom."

He had to force himself across the floor so he could kiss the top of her head, her hair sticky with so much hairspray she was a threat to the ozone.

"You will come to lunch this weekend?" Mom said.

"I'll …" Jake bit off the word *try*.

"I hope to see you then."

Once she was gone, Jake flicked the coffee pot on, then switched it back off. He grabbed a couple of bottles of Two Birds instead, and slid one across the bar to Milo.

"Man!" Milo said.

They toasted and drank – or at least Milo drank, a discretionary sip before he rested his bottle on the bar; Jake gulped half of it down. He slammed the bottle on the bar, and thought about how he'd like another – or even another three or four. This was how Dad must've started.

"You should've told her about Sherry," Milo said. "Beautiful woman. Classy – well, except for her taste in you. And professional."

Jake averted his gaze from Milo.

"Sherry's not a professional? I thought you said she was a book editor."

"I don't know where that's going."

"You've seen her twice, which is twice as long as your other relationships."

"My life is more than a series of one-night stands."

"Yeah, there are three-night stands, and four-night stands. And the fuckbuddies. Yet there's not an iota of commitment to any of them. No relationship whatsoever. But I can tell by the way you talk about this one, she's different."

"She's not that different."

"Why're you denying it? It's all right."

"Okay. You know what I like about her?"

Milo held out his arms, as if to say, *Enlighten me.*

"I like the way she fucks."

"Geez, Jake, you're the sophisticate."

"Hey, don't tell me relationships don't involve physical chemistry. Don't tell me you would've married Alice if she was terrible in bed."

"All right," Milo nodded, "I'll give you that. But I don't think of it just as crass as *fucking*. You go beyond that in a relationship. Do you get that?"

"Sure," Jake said much too quickly, because Milo always talked like this. People could call the act whatever they liked. It didn't change what it was, nor did it assign it any greater importance.

"So, what's this one do for you?" Milo asked.

"There are three types of fucks."

Milo chuckled with some incredulity.

"I'm serious. The first type: they lay there, and just enjoy being fucked."

"That's beautiful, man. We should put that on a card: *Thank you for lying there.*"

"Goes both ways. Some men just lie there. They're just not good at sex – they wait for things to happen. Second type: they're in sync with you. It's like—"

"Love?"

"Well, that's what you tell me. I wouldn't know. But it can be just as lame. You move to the other person's expectations – lame as fuck."

"It's synchronicity, like dancing."

"A boring waltz."

"Okay. The third type?"

"You fuck them, and they fuck you right back – it's like you're each trying to get the other to surrender. But neither of you give in – at least not permanently. That's Sherry."

"All right, let me put this to you: from what you're saying, you're enjoying the physical side more than you have with any other woman. That could still be the foundation for a relationship."

"We're not gonna have a relationship. She's married."

Milo spluttered his beer over the bar. Jake grabbed a sponge to wipe it up, but Milo used one clean elbow of his coveralls.

"Is she divorcing?" he asked.

"No."

"Is she separating?"

"Nope."

"Does she have an open relationship?"

"Not as far as I know."

"Then …?"

"She's unhappy."

"So? I'm unhappy half the time. *That's* marriage. It's not a fairy tale."

"You worry too much."

"You've done this before – aggrieved husbands showing up at bars you've worked. Remember that big guy, that big, big guy who showed up with the gun?"

"I can take care of myself."

"Security took care of him. How many altercations like that have you had?"

"It's only three."

"*Six.*"

"That many?" Jake feigned surprised. It was sixteen. Milo had seen only six and was still concerned. For Jake, it had grown so normalized it had become meaningless. He wasn't responsible for how other people responded – that was their problem. And the situations were easy enough to defuse, or divert. Most partners lost their belligerence anyway when they saw him.

"That many. You even had that lesbian confront you in that restaurant. I think you like the drama."

Jake snorted. He hated the drama. Pointless and overdone. He liked that he could throw married women back. Or the husband would reclaim them. Or they would meet halfway, which was just fine

– that was as much distance as he needed them to be from him. These were trysts with inbuilt expiration dates.

"You're making too much of it," he said.

"I'm serious."

"I don't know if I'll see her again."

"Jake, come on."

"I don't."

Milo popped up from his stool. "I've got to go back to work." He took one last drink. "Think about what I've said, huh? Please? For me."

"Sure."

But even as Jake made the vow, he knew he was lying.

18.

Sherry picked up her Saab, then sped into the city, performing the calculations for how late she'd be to the launch. Each of Skip's launches had grown progressively more redundant, padded with meaningless hobnobbing and self-important preamble. It was the cost of budding fame. Sherry estimated there'd be ninety minutes of it. Skip loathed it most of all. She *wanted* to enjoy it – she did with her other authors, proud of their accomplishments. Skip, however, was a blight on any such celebration. It was something to be tolerated.

She parked her car in the underground lot of the modern office high-rise where Gray's occupied three floors – a recent move since the building they'd occupied for fifty years in what had become an industrial outskirt had suffered a litany of issues ranging from unreliable plumbing to mold to the building itself inevitably failing inspection. A hostile takeover had seen Gray's refurbished on every level – everybody but the CEO had been ousted (and he only hung on grimly), some of the staff had been turned over, and there'd been the much-needed relocation.

She rode the elevator up to the eighteenth floor. The doors dinged open to an air of reverence. They'd brought in a feng shui interior designer whose one concession to the array of partitioned desks was some colorful expressionisms hung on the walls, an immaculate kitchenette with an exhaustive range of herbal teas, and several sculptures that were meant to harmonize the working space. Sherry loved the conceit that books were made here – not the physical act, but the cultivation of the thought that went into them – but she found this new space ostentatious. As sepulchral as the old place was, at least it had character.

Given it was a Saturday morning, only a handful of staff were in: the janitor, in his blue coveralls, emptying out the bins; a couple of the designers, no doubt working overtime to get covers right; and a gangly intern – possibly fresh out of high school, or new to some tertiary education – marking up a manuscript with a green pen.

Pria was in her corner office – an office that was as simple and elegant as the woman herself. She'd been an athletic terror when she was younger, a dynamo who had dominated a variety of sports at state level, before opting to pursue a career in publishing. Although she'd turned fifty earlier in the year, she'd retained a natural beauty, curated through healthy diet, rigorous exercise, and daily meditation. Now, she smiled as Sherry knocked on the jamb, then studied her a moment.

"Very glamorous," Pria said.

"I'm on my way to Skip's launch," Sherry said, as she lay Luis's manuscript on Pria's desk.

Pria frowned. "Something else about you, though – a radiance. You're not pregnant, are you?"

"I hope not."

Pria leaned back in her chair. "I feel something about you."

And that was also Pria – not only natural, but holistic. She'd once taken Sherry to a yoga retreat, where they'd eaten nothing but rice for a week, performed yoga five times a day, and had group chats about karmic reparation. Sherry had wilted under the tedium. The coup de grâce had been a sauna where Sherry had feared, for an instant, that Pria had made a pass at her – a hand on Sherry's thigh. Feeling Sherry tense, Pria had wordlessly lifted her hand. Sherry didn't know if she'd misread the situation, but Pria hadn't asked her to any sort of retreat again, and the matter had been locked away, never to be discussed.

"Are you eating healthier?" Pria said.

"Same as always."

"Exercising more?"

"No." Sherry drew the word out, like it was a bandage to cover the wound of her life – she hadn't been exercising. Unless sex counted. And the sex she'd been having was much more vigorous – and enjoyable – than exercise.

"Perhaps you've discovered my secret to remaining young and vital."

"I think the secret, if anything, is getting that," Sherry pointed at Luis's manuscript, "out of my life."

"Ah yes, Luis's latest." Pria spun the manuscript around and flicked through the pages, nodding every now and again. "Excellent, excellent, but I'd expect nothing less from you." She closed the manuscript. "An opening is coming up."

"For …?"

"My job."

"You're leaving?"

"I'm …"

Pria pointed a single finger at the ceiling – a promotion. Rumblings that the CEO, Randolph Lippincott – a man who'd been at Gray's since its foundation five decades earlier – was about to retire had flittered through the offices, although those rumors had run recurringly over the last three years, especially whenever there'd been administrative upheaval. Some suggested the only way they'd pry Lippincott out of his office was when they carried him out on a gurney, the sheet pulled over his face.

"Is it official?" Sherry asked.

Pria nodded.

"Congratulations!"

"Thank you. And with that being the case, I'm happy to recommend you as the fiction publisher – if you want the position? Your work has always been exemplary, you've transformed some of our most problematic manuscripts into gems, and I think we'll excel with you in charge of our fiction. What do you say?"

Sherry almost laughed. "Yes!"

"Excellent! It comes with a substantial salary bump, and you'll be truly able to determine the direction we take – already, I think you have a better handle on that than me."

"You're too kind —"

"Accept the praise, Sherry. I'm surprised you haven't been head-hunted already for such a position, but now you'll have the biggest and best. Let's keep this quiet, though, until," Pria pointed to the ceiling again, "formally announces his retirement. As for this," she planted her hands on Luis's manuscript, "I hope this is worth the pain Luis is."

"It's ... something – brilliant, in its way."

"Luis *is* brilliant. Unquestioningly. But he's not entirely commercial and, unfortunately, that's the reality of our business. Sometimes, I think he would fare better with a smaller publisher – a boutique publisher who would identify with his voice."

"I think that'll be his breakthrough," Sherry said. "He has the critical acclaim. That'll be the commercial correlation."

"Well, we can hope, but I remain to be convinced. Speaking of breakthroughs, how's Skip doing with the new one?"

Sherry thought about Skip's hopelessness at the keyboard and arched her brows.

"That well?" Pria said.

"I think he's a little bit stuck."

"We feel Skip's on the cusp of something magnificent – the last book spent two weeks in the *New York Times* bestseller list. *Cold Enterprise* could be something stratospheric. And the next one … well, he shouldn't stress. If he goes as we're projecting, his next one could be his laundry list and it'd sell."

"He'd still stress," Sherry said.

A knock at the door interrupted them – the intern, coming in shyly with a sheaf of rumpled paper. He clutched them to his chest, as if afraid they might try and flee. His eyes shifted back and forth, unable to meet Pria's, or – and even though Sherry smiled at him – her own.

"I–I finished that p–proofing," he said.

"Thank you, Ben. This is Sherry, one of our senior editors – although she often works off-site. She handles several of our bestselling authors, and a stable of upcoming authors."

"Oh, w–wow," Ben said.

"Ben's interning with us as part of his university requirement," Pria said. "He would like to become an editor."

"Nice to meet you," Sherry said, as she shook a hand that was surprisingly large and strong, given Ben looked like a harsh word would wilt him.

"Ben's work has shown real promise," Pria said. "Particularly his editing."

Ben lowered his head sheepishly.

"Pria taught me everything I know," Sherry said. "She was my mentor – in my professional and personal life. You could have no better teacher." She rose from her chair. "Now, if you'll excuse me, I really should be going – the launch and all."

Pria tilted her head and her eyes almost seemed to light up with realization. "And all?" she said.

The heat flushed into Sherry's cheeks. "You won't be joining us?" she asked as a means of diverting.

"You're representative enough for us, Sherry. And given your possible future, it's worth you being the face of Gray's."

"Now there's a thought."

"Have fun," Pria said.

"I'll try," Sherry said.

19.

The Grande Reception was a venue better suited to state functions, the hall enormous with large, curtained windows, Greek columns (with sculpted cherubs up the top) supporting the high ceiling, and a striped, black marble floor. Placards for *Cold*

Enterprise flanked the entry, sentries that greeted and – through sheer size – tried to awe every attendee.

Skip accosted a drinks waiter, only to find she was carrying flutes of champagne. He instructed her to get him a beer, corrected that to *two* beers, and then shrank into himself, surreptitiously popping two Xanax into his mouth and crunching on them like they were breath mints.

Around him, the crowd – replete in their finery – raved about how good *Cold Enterprise* was, unaware that its very author lurked amongst them. The praise could've been flattering, but it was uninformed gushing for the sake of gushing so they could all be part of the same literary elitism, which ultimately amounted to a whirlpool of shit.

A different waiter found Skip and delivered two beers – this waiter was young, with a round face and snub nose that might've been flattened with a frying pan had he been a cartoon character. His heavy-lidded eyes suggested a lack of alertness, if not dim-wittedness, but they grew wide when he saw Skip – here was somebody who recognized him, and deferred to him with genuine reverence.

"I loved your book!" the waiter said. "Stayed up all night reading it. It's ... mind-blowing."

Skip raised a beer in acknowledgment. Here was *real* praise – naïve and cliché. The waiter was too stupid to be pretentious and too innocent to be beguiling. It was an unfair juxtaposition – those articulate enough to speak eloquently only spoke disingenuously, while those who expressed verisimilitude were too overwhelmed to offer anything but tired old tripe.

"I want to write," the waiter said.

So there it was – he was a romantic. Unsurprising.

"Is there anything you could suggest for me?"

"Write," Skip told him.

The waiter blinked – apparently that was his fallback for surprise. Skip wasn't sure why *write* was such flabbergasting advice. Too many of these romantics thought the experience was magical, that it was just a case of sitting down and it all blissfully poured out – perfect words, perfect sentences, perfect story, perfect reviews, perfect sales, perfect everything. Skip envied that innocence.

"Read lots," he said, "study whatever you want, but you learn best by writing over and over. Get feedback, too, from people who understand what you're doing, but who'll be honest and constructive. And did I tell you to read *lots*? Don't ever stop reading. But, other than that ... *write*. Nothing ever gets finished by talking about it."

As if the collective pomposity had propagated to spontaneously give birth, Tyson slid out from the crowd, almost glowing – suit too shiny, skin too bronzed, teeth too white, smarm too smarmy. He put a hand on the waiter's back and smoothly steered him away.

"A champagne, thank you," Tyson told him.

"Get me another two beers, too," Skip added.

"Skip, you have a speech to make."

"And I'll make it."

Skip nodded at the departing waiter. The waiter grinned back, bumped into several guests, apologized profusely, and then lumbered onward. He had a meaningless anecdote now that would probably be embellished with each retelling, but good for him. At least it was something he could potentially build upon.

"How about we stay level-headed?" Tyson asked, and reached for Skip's beers.

Skip swung away from him. "No, okay? *No*. You know how I hate these things."

"Interesting way to treat your readers."

"These people aren't my readers. They're industry leeches."

"That's charming, Skip."

"These people are so mindless in their collective enthusiasm you shudder to challenge them for fear that one speck of original thought will see you condemned as some free-thinking anarchist.

They're the *liternazi*, incestuous and inbred, commending one another for their brilliance, reveling in their myopia and, by virtue of that, perpetuating mediocrity."

"Sounds like you've rehearsed that for a while."

"Me? Never."

"Are you about done then?"

"I'd rather do a book-signing than one of these things any day."

"Good, because you have that Monday – remember?"

Skip was about to be indignant for the sake of being indignant but stopped himself. Another possibility troubled him: was the indignation just another facet of the affectation he'd created? Maybe all these people were simply a byproduct of his endeavors. That would make sense.

"I'm impressed," Tyson said. "I expected a protest."

"Not me," Skip said. He finished one beer, reached behind a curtain, and planted the empty glass on a windowsill.

"How about some champagne instead?" Tyson asked. "At least don't be so common."

"I like being common. Keeps me grounded."

"You're anything *but* grounded."

"I *am* grounded."

"And you're anything but common."

"I am common."

"You're misanthropic."

"But a good misanthropic," Skip said airily. "The sort who'd be the star of a TV show – you know, the author who solves mysteries in his spare time."

"They did that with that old TV series *Murder She Wrote*."

"But she wasn't misanthropic. Get on that, will you?"

"Could you take something seriously?"

"I'm taking my beer seriously." Skip gulped half of it down.

Tyson took a deep breath. "Where's Sherry?"

"Had to pick up her car, and then drop off Luis's manuscript."

"How're things between you and her?"

"Why do you ask?"

"Because I'm waiting on pages from your next book, Skip, and I'm not getting them. So, I'm wondering if something's distracting you."

The waiter returned with the champagne and two beers on a tray. Skip finished his second beer, put the empty on the tray, and grabbed the replacements. Tyson took his champagne. The waiter stood there, beaming, like he was a dog awaiting a treat. Skip guzzled down one of the beers and handed the empty back to the waiter.

"Thank you," Tyson said.

"Should I bring—?" the waiter said.

"Sure," Skip said.

"No." Tyson drew a twenty from his pocket and stuffed it in the waiter's pocket. "I'm sure you have other people to serve."

"Thank you." The waiter nodded and left.

"We were talking about Sherry—" Tyson said.

"Sherry loves me. Everybody loves me."

"I don't love you, Skip."

"You love me most of all. Except for the whole Sherry thing. You need to stop nit-picking. You had a thing—"

"We didn't really have a thing—"

"—it didn't work out—"

"We had a brief relation—"

"—and now you have to let go of the grudge."

"There's no grudge. The beer's made you boisterous."

"Possibly. But you've always been guarded about Sherry."

"Skip, I've represented you through three books, negotiated a killer deal for your next three, and am trying to get you a juicy screenwriting deal."

"It's the lines, Tyson, the lines. You and I, that's professional. You and Sherry, that's personal. But the lines, Tyson, they don't cross. Anyway, you mightn't love me, but you do like me."

"I'm starting not to."

"Life's tough that way."

"Skip?"

"Yeah?"

"Go mingle."

20.

Hot water sprayed over Jake's face and ran down his chest. Muscles loosened and tensions swirled down the drain, taking Milo's admonitions and Mom's complaints with them. There was nothing now: no stress, no anxieties, nothing but what he had to do – or at least that's what he tried to tell himself. The release didn't quite come the way it used to. He used to be able to enter a zone, like when he played football. All that mattered was what he was focused on. But now there was a sliver of unease trembling away.

The crevice – from the two tiles that had broken off when he'd fucked Sherry in the shower – drew his attention. He traced his fingers over the jagged concrete, hoping this wasn't a sign of The Rap's fragility – it *was* an old building, and he'd eagerly signed up because the loft meant he could live right above work. Maybe the fallen tiles were a sign of something greater. No, that was stupid. He shuddered but couldn't shake the fear.

Something thumped downstairs. Jake lifted his head to listen. What had happened after Milo had left? Jake couldn't remember locking the door – a silly mistake, but he had been rattled by Milo's rebuke and Mom's condemnations.

Jake got out of the shower, slung a towel around his waist, and fetched the baseball bat he kept under his bed. Footsteps echoed from the bar and floated up the chute of the stairwell. Somebody *was* down there. He crept down the stairs, reached for the door into the bar, shoved it open, and leaped out, brandishing his bat.

His towel unfurled and bundled around his ankles.

Sherry stood at the bar, dressed in this little pink thing, like she might be going out for cocktails. She had a beer in hand – a Peroni she'd grabbed from the fridge. Her eyes roved his body and fixed on his crotch.

"Nice bat," she said.

Jake traipsed naked to the front door. "Was this unlocked?"

"Yep."

Jake locked the door, then turned to Sherry.

"Aren't you a little overdressed?" he said.

Sherry got up from her stool, pulled down the left strap of her dress, and then the right. The dress slid down her naked breasts and caught on her hips. She hooked her thumbs into it, easing it over her white lace underwear, and slid it down her thighs until it crumpled around her ankles. She stepped out of it, casually folded it, and draped it over a stool.

"I enjoy a challenge," she said.

She eased a finger down from his chest, over his belly, and into the tangle of his pubic hair. His cock – always ahead of his own ability to process a situation – sprung up to meet her palm in a handshake. Jake lifted a thumb over his shoulder to indicate the people walking past outside.

"The windows ..."

"Didn't stop you the other night."

"That *was* night."

Sherry stroked his cock, then cupped his balls in her hand. "You sure you need these?" she said.

Jake backed into the door as she knelt and took him in her mouth. The bat fell from his limp grasp. The wrongness of the situation jarred through his mind, and that had never happened before when sex had been involved. Mom had just been in here. He could still feel her presence. But, as Sherry's head bobbed back and forth, her lips tethered his will to her ministrations.

He dragged her up by the arm, spun her, and shoved her against the door so that her buttocks sprang back into his crotch. She glanced over her shoulder, startled. He tore off her underwear and tossed them away. She laughed – a triumphant laugh that slowed into a moan when he thrust into her, harder than he should've. But she was ready. He fucked her against the door, driving into her until he was lifting her onto her tiptoes with each thrust.

Jake's hands tightened around Sherry's slender hips. She bent at the waist, her hands splayed against the door as it rattled in the jamb. Her legs trembled. Jake could see her capitulating – except for the way she propelled against him to meet every thrust, like a prize fighter absorbing an opponent's best blows before counter-attacking.

Then he was coming before he could stop himself, coming sooner than he was accustomed to, and he grunted into her neck and clutched at her breasts, holding on because he was afraid if he didn't, he'd collapse to the floor.

21.

Skip scribbled an inane message (*Thanks for being a fan! Hope you enjoy the Enterprise*) across the title page, followed by his ungainly signature. The young blonde he handed the book back to was gorgeous; she smiled and mumbled a thank you. Coming out of high school, Skip yearned for this sort of attention, if not reverence, but now that it happened regularly he recognized it as flattering but gratuitous. *And* sycophantic. He turned away – the blonde's smile crumbling – and bumped into Luis.

It was, in fact, hard to miss Luis, given the mishmash of his attire. He wore an old cord blazer and cargos, one side of his denim shirt wasn't tucked in, and his socks, as well as his shoes, were mismatched. His big blue bow tie might've belonged to a clown. The only symmetry was the glass of champagne in each hand.

"Luis!" Skip said. "Surprised to see you here."

Luis held up his champagne glasses. "Free drinks." Then he scowled. "And *they* suggest I come. Said good exposure."

They. Followed by publicity. That could only mean the publisher, Gray's. They'd requested (emphatically) that he attended Luis's launch two years ago. There'd been other authors, other launches. *Exposure,* they'd told him – fraternize with the cliques and in-crowds because it was meant to help with how his books would be received. Skip hated the politics behind all of it. It was little wonder such doubt preoccupied him.

"How's the book coming?" he asked.

"Book done," Luis said, scowling. "Finished. Good riddance."

"What's it called? 'The Single Side of Duality'?"

"They keep changing."

"What do you call it?"

"Shit."

"Really?

"It be worse, if not for Sherry."

"She's obviously trying to get you through it, given how much time she's spent with you recently."

"Recently? Once."

"Once?"

"Once." Luis nodded, his frizzy hair bouncing like sprung coils.

"When?"

Luis gulped down the champagne from one of the flutes. "I don't know."

"How can you not know?"

"I don't."

"Think."

Luis frowned. "That night it rained."

"Not last night? Or the night before?"

Luis eyes tilted up to the left. "Once, to finish changes." He downed his second champagne flute, unceremoniously ditched both glasses in a nearby pot plant, then shook his hands as if he was trying to shake any trace from them.

"And that was it?" Skip asked. "You're sure?"

"Am sure."

"You're—"

"That was the last time," Luis said. "No more. Last time."

Before Skip could consider it further, Tyson sidled out of the crowd in that way where he seemed to materialize, although it was likelier he'd waited on the fringe, listening, timing his appearance.

"Luis!" he said.

He thrust out his hand. Luis scowled at it. Tyson lowered his hand.

"How's your representation treating you?" he asked.

"Like flies on swirl of dog shit, baking in sun."

"What does that mean?"

"Surely you know, Mason."

"Tyson."

"I'm Luis."

"No, I'm Tyson. Tyson Valance. And if you're thinking of new management – management with a personal touch – I can help you with that. Who're you with? Unified Artists?"

"Maybe. I think. I need drink." Luis bundled into the crowd.

Tyson took the hand he'd offered in handshake and rested it on Skip's shoulder. "Where the hell's Sherry?" he said. "We need to get this started!"

Skip shrugged. It was a good question.

22.

Sherry took a shower in tepid water, washing quickly from the waist down. She could feel Jake's ejaculate sticky and resistant inside her. He hadn't done this before, hadn't come inside her, always withdrawing instead, and splashing her belly, or lower back, like he was staking a claim over her. It was juvenile, but there was something appealing about that simplicity – something almost intoxicating about how wholly he wanted to possess her, like her first high school boyfriend who'd doted on her until he'd sacrificed all his friends. It meant something to be wanted *that* much. As if to prove this in the best way he knew how, Jake tried to get in the shower, but she held him out – she was going to be late.

Once she was done, she checked her hair and make-up in the mirror – she had to prop up her hair the best she could and had to retouch her make-up. Jake hugged her from behind, his right hand caressing her hip. He kissed her cheek, then moved for her lips. She kissed him back, and felt how easy it would be to let go now, everything else be damned. His other hand cupped her breast, but she reluctantly caught his wrist to halt him.

"You could stay," he said.

"I'd like to."

"Then do it."

"People are waiting."

"Sorry about letting go like that." Jake kissed her neck.

"It's okay," she told him.

That was the other thing. He'd been quick. *Premature.* That was flattering in itself, but entirely unsatisfying.

She used a fresh towel to pat herself dry. He spun her and clawed his hands into her buttocks like he might lift her from her feet and sit her on the bathroom sink. She planted her palms in his chest and pushed him back, needing to defuse this before he took control and she lost it.

"I need to go," she said.

"Where?"

"Book launch."

"Blow it off."

"I can't."

"Sure you can."

"Can't all be about the fun." Sherry tugged playfully on his cock. "Got to work."

"All work and no play …"

"That's life."

"How can you have an author more important than me?"

"It's my husband."

Jake frowned. "How can you have an author more important than me?"

Sherry chuckled.

Jake's hands tightened on her hips. "You can't blow it off?"

"He'll be drunk by the end of it. Maybe I'll try come back later."

Sherry slithered out of his embrace, then led him down to the bar. She found her dress, stepped back into it, and smoothed it out. Her underwear was torn and unsalvageable. Jake plucked them out of her hand, grinned, and dangled from one finger.

"You're a fiend," she said.

"You like fiends."

"That's the second set that's been a casualty to this bar. Did you find my others?"

"Uh uh."

She made her way to the door. Jake nimbly intercepted her; he held her underwear in one hand the way he might hold a leash. He ran the other hand under her dress and into her public mound. She arched into him and kissed him. He ran kisses down her neck, and onto her chest.

"I'll be back," she said.

She shot from The Rap and out to the parking lot. By the time she'd gotten to her car, he was already at the second-story window, still naked, and still holding her torn underwear. He lifted a finger to his temple – a salute. She waved, then sank into her car. Her crotch felt sticky – the price of a hasty shower. She hoped it didn't stain through her dress.

On the drive up, she expected something would hit – guilt, remorse, even lust. But a flat calm prevailed. Something had to be wrong, although it had been like this when she'd left Tyson for Skip. Of course, she and Tyson had gone on a handful of dates, and it had never felt right. She'd been married to Skip for five years, although most of the time it felt as if she was his babysitter.

Parking was sparse at the Grande, and she could only find a spot at the very topmost corner of the lot. She sprang out of her car and broke into a canter, the straps of her shoes cutting into her heels, and her breasts threatening to bounce from her dress. The absence of a bra was stupid – titillation for Jake. But she felt exposed now. She forced herself to a walk. The last thing she needed was to be disheveled. Alibis flittered through her head. Pria wanted to talk. That's all it came down to. Skip wouldn't check.

Sherry crept into the reception; the huddled audience was a pastiche of drab suits and bright elegant gowns – and far more than she would've anticipated. Their silence held a reverence usually reserved for the pious. Skip, of course, was anything but – he stood on the stage at the front, slumped in that lackadaisical way he carried himself in public.

"One of the truths about writing – or at least my writing – is that desire to lose myself in my story," he was saying. "And it's not easy to lose myself. I *try*."

Some of the audience tittered, like they were being let in on some great confidence. Sherry tried to pick her way through to the front, but the crowd were too dense. The numbers were a sign of Skip's exploding popularity. She retreated to the bar at the back, sat on a stool, and signaled for a champagne.

"When I sit down to write," Skip said, "that blank page an unassailable wall, that blinking cursor a mocking sentry, I wonder, how do I get through? Sometimes I don't. I butt my head against the wall and that cursor pops with laughter. Other times, I skirt the edges, and get glimpses of what could be. And sometimes, I sneak through and see the people I'm writing about and experience the events they're experiencing. Then I report what they're doing as best as I can."

He paused, eyes closed, and swayed. He'd been drinking – that was a given. Sherry wondered *how* much. Tyson might've tried to contain him but Tyson held little authority over Skip. Skip would've done the opposite of anything Tyson asked just to annoy him. She would've been a better chaperone. But there it was again – her role in this marriage.

The silence continued. Some in the crowd murmured, suspecting no doubt that Skip had fallen asleep on his feet, or possibly passed into a drunken stupor – he had that reputation for drinking, and his behavior had never disabused anybody of the notion. It was because when he did drink, he was the fun drunk – well, that was his public side. They didn't see him privately when he sank into melancholy, when he questioned his self-worth, when he queried his whole existence.

"But you know what?" Skip's eyes snapped open. "Even when I believe I've gotten it right, even after I've sat there countless hours revising, I rely on one person above all others."

He scoured the assemblage. Sherry rose on her stool, balanced on one of the struts, and held up her glass. He spotted her, nodded, and straightened. Sherry could imagine that right then, he heard her voice in his ear, *Don't slouch!*

"To my ... brilliant ... wife," he said, gesturing expansively toward her, "and brillianter editor – yes, *brillianter* isn't a word, but it'll do for this purpose. I see a world when I write. When she edits me, she makes me see a universe."

His praise stirred a token of affection for him, but only a token, and underlying that, some vestige of guilt jagged in, flaring spectacularly, nauseatingly, but ultimately simmering to little more than uneasiness. It should've been worse. If this was a story, she would've challenged the author to explore the depth of guilt a character *should* be feeling. But it was pitiable and, pathetically, a big reason for that was sex with Jake. Something as primal as his desire for her overrode everything else.

Everybody turned to look at her, and for a moment Sherry was sure they were condemning. They *knew*. She wore her betrayal on her face. And they could not believe she could cheat on somebody as amazing, as endearing, as insightful as Skip.

Sherry geared down her apprehensiveness as the audience broke into thunderous applause. Skip had moved them. He was capable of that as an author. Talking about writing humanized him. And this was how they'd connected, and what they'd built their relationship upon. But while these connections had been as stunning and incendiary and wowing as fireworks, they had the same lifespan.

Sherry slid gracefully from the stool, her feet finding the floor, and as she lifted her glass in acknowledgment, she felt something small and sticky ooze out from her, some bit of Jake that had escaped her quick shower.

She had to brace herself from fleeing to find the toilet, and instead took a step forward, nodded, smiled, and sipped from the champagne, feeling as if every set of eyes condemned her, and the uncharacteristic grin from Skip was all-knowing, while the slug of cum eked down the inside of her leg.

23.

Skip hopped down into the clapping audience and, when it became clear he wanted to break his way through, they parted, and patted him on the back and shook his hand or kissed him on the cheek. His reciprocation was token, but they understood, because this was such a grand and romantic moment that they didn't want to intrude; they just wanted to be part of it, however fleetingly.

Sherry waited, shifting from one leg to the other, like a shy schoolgirl overwhelmed by getting to talk with her crush. She was so demure and unsophisticated in this very moment, so vulnerable, that he hugged her and kissed her with a fierceness he hadn't expressed for years. Wolf whistles and cheers punctuated the applause. Then the analytical part of Skip's mind asserted itself. She smelled like Sherry – the vanilla perfume, that tangy hairspray she overused, the soft, musky deodorant ... and was that something else? Sweat?

"You're late," he said.

"Pria," Sherry said.

The applause transformed into chatter as the audience finally recognized the show was over, and they dispersed into their small social clusters. Then an arm came around each of Skip and Sherry – Tyson, grinning.

"Magnificent, Skip!" he said. "What a showman you are! I couldn't have scripted that better. And you, Sherry," he examined her from head to toe and back again, that overly smooth forehead trying to crease through a façade of Botox, "what an entrance! You look outstanding."

"Thank you, Tyson," she said.

"Did you two plan this? You did, didn't you?" Tyson smiled. "Go on, you can tell me."

Sherry glanced at Skip, the bridge of her nose crinkling to show her disbelief. He offered nothing in return – if she would've seen it anyway, as she turned back to Tyson.

"I was in such a rush to get here, I'm going to ..." Sherry gestured to the foyer, then scooted off.

Skip eased his way to the bar, and signaled the bartender for two beers. Tyson clapped a hand on his shoulder – Tyson was big on clapping hands on shoulders and backs, like he might've been handling a ventriloquist's dummy. The bartender slid two glasses of beer across – one in front of Skip, one in front of Tyson. Skip took both of them.

"Some moderation, please," Tyson said.

"What?"

"You have books to sign. You know? People expect it of you."

"I'm fine."

"By my count, you've already had ten."

Skip finished the first beer without taking a breath.

"*Eleven.*" Tyson applied pressure to his back to get him moving. "Skip? Please."

Two tables had been set up by the window – one for Skip, the other for an attractive silver-haired woman in an overlong velvet robe from Blaise's Bookstore to sell books.

People filed past; he signed their copies in his unwieldy left hand, thanking them for coming, and telling them he hoped they enjoyed his book – platitudes that flowed unthinkingly, while he thought about Sherry's tardiness.

She joined him and leaned over to kiss him. Her forearm folded across her bodice to make sure she wasn't exposed. She was bra-less. That wasn't unusual … was it? He was embarrassed he didn't know. When they'd first gotten together, she'd go bra-less if the dress suited it. But she did wear bras. He even knew which drawer they occupied. He just wasn't sure if she wore them regularly.

The line moved on until Luis appeared, a big wet stain on his crotch and running down his right leg. He was oblivious to it, and how people frowned at him or chortled behind their hands, while others discreetly photographed or filmed him. Luis wouldn't care; plenty of such exhibits existed online, accompanied by a range of quotes from people who shared their anecdotes of interacting with him. It all added to his mystique.

He thrust a copy of *Cold Enterprise* at Skip, the cover wrinkled and dog-eared, like it was a book he'd owned years, and wet fingerprints embedded in some of the pages. Skip delicately flipped open the cover, but just as he applied his pen to the page, he paused; he could feel Sherry tense up beside him.

"You tell Pria my launch not here," Luis told her.

"I will."

"Toilet too far! Too far!"

"We can see."

"You give book?"

"I dropped it off this morning."

"I thinking—"

"No, Luis."

"You don't know what I say."

"You were thinking of making a change."

Luis lifted his head and bellowed with laughter. "You magnificent beast. Leave this bum." He thrust a hand out at Skip. "We fuck all time – maybe two-three times a week."

Skip chuckled. Because Sherry had left Tyson for Skip, Luis had ongoing banter that she'd leave

Skip for him. When Luis had first started joking about it several years ago, Skip had been jealous. Sherry appreciated intelligence. While Luis's broken English might fool people into thinking he was uneducated, he was a genius (and Skip suspected Luis's grasp of English was nowhere near as clumsy as he perpetuated, and much of his iconoclasm was theatre). But while Sherry respected Luis, she'd never been drawn to him.

"That's a tantalizing offer," she said, "but I'm going to have to decline."

"You sleep on it."

Skip, mindless platitude written, held the book out.

Luis seized it. "Any good?"

"I hope."

Luis shoved the book in his pocket. "I look forward to many toilet reads." He stumbled off in the direction of the bar.

"He been here long?" Sherry said.

"First time I've seen him," Skip said.

"Looks well-oiled."

Skip watched for any change in her demeanor, for any softening in her face, for any relaxation in her posture, but she was stoic, her head tilted low, eye lashes dark and long, those pouty lips insinuating a smile that she knew something he didn't.

The line proceeded, and he continued to sign, continued to drink, as he explored the possibilities as to why Sherry had lied about seeing Luis. She'd banked on a dumb alibi because Luis rarely came out in public. His appearance was one of those bizarre happenstances that unlocked an insane chain of events.

Once there were no more books to sign, Skip excused himself, hit the toilets and took two Xanax. When he came back, he found the crowd had thinned, so it was easy to spot Sherry talking to a tall, pleasant-faced man in an awful woolen vest, *Cold Enterprise* tucked under his arm.

Skip grabbed a couple of beers and gulped one down. He left the glass on the bar, then lumbered toward Sherry, sliding a territorial arm around her waist.

"And here he is!" the tall man said. He lifted *Cold Enterprise*. "Looking forward to this; loved your others." He thrust one hand forward. "Oliver Townsend – Palette Publishing."

Skip shook his hand. He wasn't good with first impressions. Usually, imagination took over. Oliver wasn't handsome or ugly, he was tall but not big or threatening, and his manner wasn't overt or sly – he was so middle-ground on everything, so spectacularly bland, that were he a character Skip wouldn't know how to describe him. The only thing that had any identity was that woolen vest, and an awful aqua blazer with leather patches on the elbows that he had folded over one forearm.

"I'm trying to poach your wife over to Palette," Oliver said. "We're tiny compared to Gray's, but we're growing fast. Especially if we could steal you also, Skip."

Tyson slid into the perimeter of their trio, as if professional impropriety had summoned him. "Tyson Valance, Skip's agent," he said. "Now what's this about stealing?"

Oliver laughed. "Nice to meet you, Tyson."

"I might let the adults talk and get myself a drink," Skip said.

"You have a drink in your hand," Oliver said.

Skip downed his beer.

"I stand corrected."

Skip retreated to the bar. Now the formalities were done and he was left to his own devices, left to being himself, the typical social unease ramped up. It had been there in school and, to his surprise, had gotten worse as he'd grown more successful. This discourse had never come naturally to him – unless he'd had a few to drink, and it was about a topic that genuinely interested him. Otherwise, he was happy to play the fool.

He ordered two more beers, and then another two, and then two more. An arm clamped down on his back, and a hand gripped his shoulder – an overt familiarity that could only be Tyson.

"Oliver Townsend raves about you," he said. "We should keep an eye on Palette in the future."

Skip swiveled on his stool and almost slipped off. Tyson – sure enough, Tyson – caught him and steadied him.

"Whoa!" Tyson said. "I think you might've had one or two too many."

He eased Skip from the stool and signaled to Sherry. She skirted across the hardwood floor, the hem of her dress bouncing, and weaved her arm around Skip. Skip kissed her cheek. Her nose wrinkled in distaste – no doubt he stunk of beer. Tyson clamped that big hand down the middle of Skip's back.

They escorted him wordlessly to the car. He closed his eyes as sleep beckoned him. Sherry's keys jingled. A door opened. Tyson maneuvered him down, down, until Skip recoiled at the cloying pineapple freshener hanging from the rearview mirror. His head lolled against the headrest. The door slammed closed. The pineapple scent thickened. Skip heard Sherry's heels circle around to the other side.

"Sherry!" Tyson's voice low but insistent.

Skip tried to blink his drowsiness away. The ghostliness of Sherry's arms appeared outside the driver's window. She reached for the door handle. Tyson's big frame appeared behind her. Skip's heart thumped. He closed his eyes, head cocked so his ear was pointed to them, like a radar dish turned to farm a signal.

"I need to talk to you," Tyson said, his voice hushed.

"I have to take Skip home."

"You can spare a minute," Tyson said. "He's asleep."

"Make it quick."

"Are you screwing around on Skip?"

"*What?*"

"When did you stop wearing underwear?"

"What sort of judgment is that?" Sherry's hand scraped against the door handle.

"When we were going out and you first hooked up with Skip – and by *hooked up* I mean *fucked him* –"

"How dare you!"

"No, Sherry, *how dare you*. You fucked him, then came to see me – not that I knew you'd fucked him. This is what I pieced together later when I was piecing myself together. But you showed up to dinner, broke up with me, and as you got up, I marveled at the lack of a panty-line in your skirt.

And when I saw you show up today – late and flustered – that was the memory that leaped to mind."

"You're bitter, Tyson."

"Bitter doesn't make me unobservant. *Or* wrong. I don't want you hurting Skip – not because I particularly care about your relationship. There's a salacious side to you, Sherry. I learned that the hard way. But Skip could be a great writer. *Phenomenal.* I'd like to see him become *that* author. It worries me that if you hurt him, it hurts his work."

"You God-damned mercenary."

"I am what I am, Sherry, whatever you may think of me. I've never pretended to be anything else. But you? As an editor, you manipulate the material to produce the results you want."

"Screw you, Tyson."

The door opened and Sherry fell into the car. She slammed the door closed, started the engine, then reached across Skip. He felt her neck under his face and the warmth of her skin. He wanted to kiss her then – just once, gently, to let her know that it was okay, even though by the sounds of it, it totally wasn't. She yanked the seatbelt down and buckled him in, then lifted herself back into her seat.

Then she put the car into DRIVE.

24.

A short brunette in an overly tight lime dress plonked herself on a stool by the bar and grinned at Jake. She was late twenties maybe, or possibly even in her thirties given the lines extending from her eyes. The dress was a throwback to her younger days – she still had a great figure, despite the ripples of fat running down her stomach like a range of unambitious hills. She indulged when it came to junk food, and didn't have time to take care of herself – at least not properly. Single mom. That was the narrative that unfurled in Jake's head. Single mom, had the kids (two, he decided) the bulk of the time, and finally got to offload them on her mother or a dick of an ex so she could have a night out and let go. She didn't even constitute prey. Her intentions beamed from her as if she was wearing neon.

He smiled back, ready to engage her as The Rap's phone rang. Milo was immediately there, before either of the bartenders, answering, "The Rap, Milo speaking." Within moments, Milo held the phone to his chest and nodded his head at Jake.

Sherry, Milo mouthed the name.

Jake took the phone, excused himself, then backed into one corner before deciding that wasn't going to be private enough. He unlocked the door to the stairwell that led up to his loft, stepped in, sat on the bottom step in darkness, and closed the door.

"Hey," he said.

"Hey," Sherry said, her voice low.

He could hear water – a bath – and imagined her naked, lying there, soaking. He stroked his erection through his jeans.

"I'm not going to be able to make it tonight," she said.

"What's wrong?"

"I've had some trouble …"

"With your husband?"

Sherry snorted. "He's drunk, dead to the world. Trouble with his agent. It's too stupid to go into. I'll try and catch you tomorrow."

"How about I come over?" he said.

"That wouldn't be prudent."

"You said your husband's dead to the world."

"I'm in the tub."

"In the tub?"

"Soaking in a hot bath. It's relaxing."

"I'm hard."

"You're hard?"

"I'm hard."

"I need to go—"

"I want you to touch yourself."

"Right now?"

"Gently, circling your nipple."

"Jake—"

"Go on – imagine I'm doing it."

"You really want—"

"I really want you to."

Sherry hissed. "I'm getting pointy."

"You wet?"

"I'm wet all over."

"You know where I mean."

Sherry chuckled. "Maybe."

Jake unzipped his jeans. "Imagine it's my finger finding my way between your legs."

"I shouldn't be doing this – my husband's in the next room."

"Dead to the world."

"This is wrong."

"Do it."

Sherry inhaled sharply.

"*Gently.*"

Sherry's breath was like the *rat-a-tat* of a machine gun.

"Could you imagine the head of my cock prying you open? Gently. *Teasing.*"

"Why tease me?"

"Do you want me inside you?"

"Maybe."

"Do you want me inside you?"

Sherry laughed.

"Think about me entering you, the way I fill you, my lips on your neck. Feel my face against your skin."

Sherry whimpered through a startled breath.

"Can you feel my finger against your clit, stroking you faster, until you tense up against me?"

"That feels good …"

"I'm thrusting inside you – slow and gentle."

"I don't want it slow and gentle."

"You're not in charge here."

"Aren't I?"

"I pull out from you, until my cock's almost all the way out." Jake eased his erection from his jeans and stroked himself. "Who's in charge?"

"I'm in charge."

"Do you want me inside you?"

"I very much want you inside me."

"Then who's in charge?"

"I don't know …"

"I thrust inside you – I do it hard because I want you to feel me."

Again, Sherry's strangled breath, underpinned by the rippling water.

"I thrust fast now, like I want to teach you a lesson."

"What sort of lesson?"

"I want to teach you who's in charge."

"I'm still ... in ..." The sentence tapered into a tremulous warble.

"I perch your ankles on my shoulders and thrust hard into you. My finger is still on your clit. Your body bounces against me. I fuck you harder. You know I'm in charge because you want me hard and fast until you don't know anything but my cock inside you and your body rocking—"

Sherry bit back her cry a moment too late, then her breath came heavy, evening out until it was slow and relaxed.

Jake yanked his hand from his cock as he felt close to coming, his erection a directionless rudder. If he came now he'd need to clean up. And it cheapened it, coming from masturbating – at least for him. He'd much rather have Sherry here and come inside her again or have her swallow. She hadn't done that yet. She would. He never would've envisioned her exhibiting such abandon when he first met her. She was not only somebody to be corrupted, but somebody who yearned for it. Her sex life (if not her life overall) must've been bland.

He sat back and felt a bulge in his pocket: that pair of Sherry's underwear he'd taken off her when they'd first had sex. He'd lied to her about their fate, and hadn't understood why at the time. Now he did – it was like having a little piece of her with him. He dabbed them over his forehead, then held them to his nose and inhaled. They smelled of The Rap.

"I shouldn't have done that," Sherry said.

"You're lounging in the tub of your own orgasm," Jake said.

"You're a bad influence on me."

"That's good to know."

"I need to go – the bathroom's a mess."

"Sure you can't get out tonight?"

"I'm sure."

"Okay – but I'll see you soon."

"Soon. And, Jake?"

"Yeah?"

"I'm in charge."

She hung up, leaving Jake to grin as he sniffed her underwear once more; then he shoved them in his pocket. He rose, zipped himself up, left the stairwell and went back into the bar. The brunette was still on the stool, nursing an empty lowball glass containing some melted ice, the rind of a lemon, and a cherry stem. He nodded his head in acknowledgment of her.

"Your handkerchief's poking out," she said.

"What? Oh!"

The hem of Sherry's underwear peeked from his pocket. He started to shove them back in, but then opened the drawer under the bar. The torn underwear she'd left behind today sat in there, arranged beatifically, like a priceless display at an exhibition.

Jake scrunched up the ones in his pocket and surreptitiously shoved them in the drawer. The brunette watched him with a carnivorous gleam. He hipped closed the drawer. The brunette would be easy, and a release might be something, although he felt a peculiar faithfulness to Sherry that he'd never experienced before with anybody.

"Another brandy sour?" he said.

"Sure."

He reached for a lemon to cut, then stopped. He hadn't washed since handling himself.

Shrugging, he grabbed the lemon, and started to prepare the drink.

25.

Skip sat up in bed, the prevailing dread the best remedy for inebriation. He could hear Sherry in the bath, her voice soft. Getting up, he pressed his ear to the bathroom door. He couldn't make out the words, but he could determine her tone: *playful.*

She wasn't talking to Luis.

She wasn't talking to another author.

She wasn't talking to Pria.

But she had talked to him like this, once upon a time.

He resisted the urge to charge in and confront her. All he had were his suspicions – well, they weren't even his suspicions. They were Tyson's, although they fueled Skip's own paranoia and insecurity. Tyson would have some insight given he'd been on the receiving end once. His fears couldn't just be dismissed.

Skip went back to bed and wrestled with the growing agitation. He breezed through questions of *why* Sherry might be cheating on him. He knew he could be inattentive, preoccupied, and selfish. Their sex life was spasmodic. The sex itself was good. Well, sometimes. Conversation was sparse – at least compared to the way they engaged, spoke, and interacted whenever she was editing one of his books. Their personal life once might've been passionate (or at least a good facsimile), but now it was criminally impersonal. She had needs. Plenty of motivation existed for her. If he'd been her, he would've cheated long ago. But that was *if* he'd been her. He could never imagine being the perpetrator.

If he was writing this, there would be a dramatic literary confrontation. No – that was jumping too far ahead. He had to learn more. Her phone! The other night, she'd claimed Luis had messaged about last-minute changes. If he could check her phone ... no – she was talking on it now. He needed something else and wrestled with what that until a mixture of inebriation and exhaustion finally claimed him and he fell into a fitful sleep.

Come the morning, the sound of the front door closing jolted him awake. Pain sheared through his head, his tongue was thick and furry, and his eyes stung. He lurched out of bed and blundered to the bedroom window just in time to see Sherry hurry down the drive and slip into a taxi. The taxi reversed from the drive, then disappeared down the street.

Skip stumbled downstairs, grabbed a bottle of juice from the fridge, and found his phone on the kitchen counter. He cycled through his contacts, selected Tyson's number, and rang. Tyson – as always – answered before the first ring.

"We need to talk," Skip told him.

"Shoot," Tyson said.

"In person."

"I'll be right over."

Skip took two Xanax with a breakfast of cereal, then showered. He was coming down the stairs when the doorbell rang – Tyson, as remarkably preened as always. Skip led him into the kitchen and grabbed a Singha from the fridge.

"Drink?" he asked.

"Didn't you get enough yesterday?"

"Yesterday was strictly recreational. Today is therapeutic. Sit down."

Tyson sat at the kitchen table, his smooth face inscrutable. No wonder he made such a good negotiator – he was impossible to read.

"Tell me about the affair you think Sherry's having," Skip said, taking a chair opposite Tyson.

Tyson blinked – his one concession to being startled. "Honestly, Skip, perhaps I'm being paranoid—"

"Sherry's been unavailable lately. She's faked meetings with Luis Stauss."

"Skip, I don't know what to say."

"Tell me what you know."

"At this point, it's a suspicion. A *hunch*."

"But if you knew for certain, you'd tell me."

Tyson clasped his hands in front of his waist. He nurtured that grudge against Sherry, and now he had the chance to bury her, but he was holding something back. Why?

"Absolutely," he said. "What *you* need to do is forget it. Bury yourself with work."

And there was *why* – he didn't want it to impact Skip's writing.

"You're such a dick, Tyson."

"Writing's your love, Skip. Do you really want a dramatic confrontation distracting you? If nothing else, it'd be premature without proof."

Skip sipped from his beer. He got up and gestured to the hall. "Okay, get out of here."

Tyson planted his hands on the table. "I don't think that'd be prudent, Skip. At a time like this, you really need somebody to be with you."

"I want to try get some writing done."

Tyson shot to his feet. "Of course, I'm an agent, not a psychiatrist." He headed down the hall. "You're not going to drink yourself into a stupor?"

Skip opened the front door and ushered Tyson through it.

"We could've done this on the phone, Skip. They're marvelous inventions."

"I wanted to see your face."

"You can make video calls, Skip."

"I needed you here. Before me."

"And what did you see?"

"Get out, Tyson."

Skip started to close the door.

"I can stay – really! I'll be quiet. You won't even know I'm here. I'll sit in a corner. Or I'll clean the house. I'll vacuum."

Skip closed the door, started for his study, but turned back. He swung open the door. Tyson remained there, unmoved. He grinned.

"You changed your mind! I knew you would – "

"I wanted to say if you *do* learn something and you don't tell me, you can consider our relationship at an end," Skip said. "Forget me finishing this book, forget me finishing any other book for you. Got it?"

Tyson nodded.

"Good."

"Anything else?"

"No. *Yes.* Another bottle of pills."

"Skip!"

"Do it," Skip told him.

Skip slammed the door closed and retreated to his study. He sank into his chair. Even if no affair existed, he had to be a better partner. Sherry deserved it. He remembered Lauren Hodder from high school – his one spectacular dalliance. They'd been paired together for a project and had gotten along to the point they'd started hanging out with one another. One afternoon, while studying in the library, they'd kissed. Then she'd been mocked for being with him. She'd dumped him and joined the popular kids in ridiculing him. That was high school – cruel and arbitrary. It was happening again. Sherry would leave. Find somebody more suitable. That wouldn't be hard.

He opened multiple tabs on his laptop's browser and perused the net. A restaurant. A five-star restaurant. And a hotel room. She'd suggested these things. He'd shot them down. But they could do them as early as tonight. A surprise! That was it. Despite the widening gulf, they could reach one another again – a married couple trying to rediscover their love.

But she had her lover. No. Not just a lover. It was more serious than that. She had another husband. That husband also suspected her of an affair. He lived in a different city. They had a child. No, wait – how could Sherry have hidden a pregnancy from Husband One? An adoption! Sherry was barren. Well, that's what she told Husband Two. What did she tell Husband Three? There *would* be another husband. And another. And a pregnancy – she wasn't barren as she'd first thought, but she did have difficulty conceiving. Now, the pregnancy changed everything. It was a problem. Whose baby was it? How did she sell the pregnancy to all these husbands? *Why* did all these husbands exist? What was her pathology? How did they find out about one another without it becoming silly and comedic? Or *did* they? The pregnancy was the disruption she couldn't hide. And then … Skip was racing too far ahead. Husband One. That's where it started. An inattentive selfish husband.

Skip closed the browser.

He opened his word processor.

And began to write.

26.

Sherry's hands tightened on the ceiling of the headboard. The muscles in her shoulders ached and threatened to buckle. It would be so easy to collapse face-first into Jake's bed and let him ride her with abandon. But she bucked and rolled her hips to meet his every thrust; the rhythm was instinctual, a need to counter him. She'd never had this before, something so physical that it eclipsed any intellectual or emotional connection or need. When orgasm wracked her body and flattened her finally onto the bed, she conceded to herself he'd won this one.

"You okay?" he said.

Sherry had to catch her breath before she could answer. "More than okay."

She fellated him while she recovered, then took him again and again, wanting to find that victory over him. He delighted in eliciting her most uninhibited responses. In reply, she wanted him however she could take him. He was relentless, and always ready again quickly.

When he suggested a shower, she challenged him to take her over the bathroom sink as they watched themselves in the mirror, she sweaty, reddened, and exposed in every way, while Jake, by comparison, was a beast uncaged who feasted on her helplessly. What wasn't beastly was Jake – with embarrassment – not lasting long on this occasion (Sherry caught him checking his form in the bathroom mirror), which was lucky, because Sherry didn't know how much longer she could bear him the way she was. They showered, then lay exhausted on the bed.

"I love fucking you," Jake said.

He grinned – a stupid, triumphant grin, like a teenager who might've become sexually active with a partner, and was enjoying the newfound regularity of it. Sherry couldn't work out if she found it endearing or offensive. She pictured him in the high school locker room, boasting not only about his conquests, but how they'd been achieved. He would've been that kid in school – and the girls would've forgiven him because he was gorgeous and great at sex.

"I haven't felt this with anybody else," she said. "I've spent so long dealing with writers living in their imaginations, and agents looking after their own self-interests that I've forgotten what it's like to be real. But I wonder …"

"What?"

Sherry thought about her diminishing guilt, about the way she framed her relationship to Skip as something that had always been flawed, if not outright faulty, but which she only recognized now. None of that would've have happened if not for Jake. But that apportioned to this relationship a value, an importance, that she wasn't sure he reconciled.

She sat up. "This needs to mean something, right?"

Jake flipped onto his side and ran a finger down her thigh. "But it does mean something."

"Beyond the sex. Do you see yourself with me tomorrow? Next week? Next month? Next year?"

"Whoa – hang on. This is getting serious."

The kid in the high-school locker room boasting – she saw him there again, but also imagined how cagey he would be about commitment. At that age, it was about scoring. About triumphs. That's what guys did to build themselves up in their peer groups. But this wasn't high school although, emotionally, he might still be that high-school kid.

Sherry got up and grabbed her clothes. "I need to go."

"Did I say something wrong?"

"I have a marriage, and I have a career. I'm risking my life as I know it."

"You wouldn't be here if there wasn't something wrong with that life."

He might've read her mind, but that didn't invalidate her point. She'd initially only been worried about the now, but the *now* was stretching into the future – or, at the very least, it was taking her further and further from the life she knew.

"Think about it," she said.

She dressed, although lots of things ached – her hamstrings, buttocks, belly, the middle of her back, her shoulder blades and shoulders. It was strange that just moments ago, they would've been good pains, the body reporting soreness after a good workout. But now it was something else, although she wasn't sure what. Guilt? Regret? Remorse? None of them fit exactly.

When she went downstairs, the tenderness dictated her gait and her mood had changed, although she was confused more than anything, unsure if she was overreacting, or this was a legitimate grievance to resolve.

"Are we okay?" Jake asked, as he walked her to the door.

"Yeah," she said in a flat tone.

She kissed him perfunctorily on the cheek, saw his immediate identification that she was annoyed, but before he could entreat her, she tottered out to Skip's Mustang. Sitting behind the steering wheel, she was sure Skip would notice her moving funny – well, if he noticed her at all.

He didn't.

He was in his study, typing – actually typing with that frenetic rhythm that meant his imagination was firing! Sherry leaned one way, then the other, and saw over his shoulder words materialize on the screen – real words, growing into sentences, the sentence building into paragraphs. A row of empty Singhas sat on his desk.

She was about to comment on the drinking – and the pills – but it was redundant. He'd found his way. Alone. And that's all that mattered to him – all that had ever mattered to him.

"Where'd you go?" Skip lifted his hands from the keyboard, although he didn't turn to face her.

Sherry dangled his keys so he could hear them jingle. "To get your car," she said. "You were too drunk to drive yesterday."

She waited for him to turn. He didn't.

"I'm going to fix some lunch. Do you want anything?"

Skip's typing slowed to a canter. "Surprise me."

Sherry retreated to the kitchen to the sound of his accelerating typing. So he was writing again. He was always at his best when he was writing. And most distant. The closeness came once he finished and handed her the manuscript so she could read it, scribble up possible revisions, and write-up her feedback. Then they'd engage on a level that she'd never engaged with anybody intellectually, emotionally, and even spiritually. That was the genuine attraction. The entanglement of their ideas, the fencing of their intellects, the union of their vision.

They'd bond.

They'd fuck.

But that was months away.

And a horrible basis for a relationship.

27.

The little Asian restaurant, Dumpling Haven, had been converted from what must've once been a middle-class suburban house. Some of the walls had been knocked down to combine rooms and create more space, but the architecture was definitively residential. The whole thing had become – either through necessity or design – utilitarian, right down to the heavy wooden chairs and tables. Culture wasn't big in the furnishings – just the food, which Jake had to admit was delicious.

He deftly used his chopsticks to turn a pork dumpling over and over into a shallow basin of soy sauce. His skill might've suggested he'd never used anything but chopsticks his whole life, whereas Milo relied on his fork – no matter how often he'd attempted to master the chopsticks, he claimed he just couldn't find the dexterity. It was strange, because Milo could nimbly strip and reconstruct car engines just by touch.

He twisted his fork into his noodles as if they were pasta, then slurped them up.

"Surprised you're not with Sherry tonight," he said.

"We have to navigate her husband," Jake said.

Milo snorted.

"What?"

"Nothing."

"*What?*"

Milo took a long swill from his bottle of Chang beer.

"Look, you obviously have something to say, so say it."

"Well, then, how is the great affair?"

Jake bit back on his surliness. "Why're you riding me about this?"

"I'm married," Milo said.

"And ...?"

"Every time you fuck a committed woman, I think, *What if Alice was fucking somebody else?* Brings up a lot of questions. Why's she doing it? Is it because of me? What have I done? Or what haven't I done—?"

"I get that—"

"I'd also wonder what *he* thinks of me. See, because on top of fucking her, he's fucking me over. How can you do that to another guy? *Repeatedly.* Have you ever thought about that?"

Jake hadn't, but wanted to claim he had. Milo didn't give him the chance.

"You don't care, though," he said. "You're a natural disaster, a tornado through everybody else's relationships. And why? Because you have to serve your master: your cock."

"Easy."

"It's always been the case, Jake." Milo sipped from his beer. "Do you talk about him?"

"Her husband?"

"No, your cock. *Yes,* her husband."

"He comes up sometimes."

"Like your cock. Wait, that's *all* the time."

"Very funny."

"And what comes out?"

"That he's self-obsessed." Jake pushed another dumpling into the soy sauce.

"So she's neglected?"

"I guess. She says he lives in his own little world."

"That's it?"

"Why are you so insistent about this one?"

"Jake, we *always* have this conversation. I keep hoping that my lectures will sink in, and it'll be the last time. Uh uh. So I've let it go. Difference now is you've now gotten into a relationship with the woman. This is a full-blown affair."

Which was true but didn't change anything. As he'd told Sherry, she wouldn't be with him if she was happy with her life. She'd shut up quick when he'd said that, even if she had gotten huffy. That was fine. She could play that game – women did.

"You should meet him," Milo said.

"What for?" Jake leaned back in his chair.

"To make it real for you. You do this a lot – you blunder ahead and worry about the consequences later. Worry about them now."

"Right – I'll just drive down, and knock on his front door: 'Hello, Mr. Lago. I'm fucking your wife. How are—'?"

"Lago?" Milo's face twisted. "She's an editor – her husband's the writer, Skip Lago?"

"How'd you know that?"

"Because I *do* read, Jake."

Milo took his phone from his pocket, brought up the browser, and began typing. Then he planted the phone on the table and spun it around for Jake to see: a banner showed a drawing of books crammed into a shelf until they were overflowing, along with the title in some gorgeous old typewriter-like font: **Blaise's Bookstore**.

Underneath it was a picture of a thirty-something man with disheveled hair and shadowy growth dressed in black. This was Skip – not some frazzled old guy, as Jake had imagined. Images flashed through his mind: this guy and Sherry at the altar getting married; Sherry's lips around his little cock; this guy thrusting into her, his rhythm lame, Sherry's gaze drifting to the ceiling. This guy sitting at his computer, typing, while Sherry stood in some other room, maybe looking longingly out the kitchen window or something, neglected.

He'd probably have a prissy way of speaking, too. Nerd-like. And high-pitched. Sure, it was an outdated cliché, but Jake had found truth in it during high school. The nerds did have their own way about them. There was a reason those stereotypes existed.

Jake scrolled the page down to read the copy: "'Blaise's Bookstore is proud to announce that best-selling author, Skip Lago, will be appearing Monday to sign copies of his new book, *Cold Enterprise*'."

"There you go!" Milo said.

"What do you mean there I go?"

"We should meet him. *You* should meet him."

"What do you expect me to say to him?"

"It's about making this real for you. You act like there're no consequences. Sometimes – and no offense – I wish you'd get burned because it's the only way I think you'll learn."

"Why do I need to learn? Like, why is this so necessary for you?"

"Because I want you to grow up and become an adult. You're dealing with people's feelings. You're dealing with people's lives. Did I say you were fucking him over? I'm wrong – you're fucking her over, too."

Jake slid the phone back across to Milo. Sherry *was* growing on him – well, that was the only way he could rationalize the continuing attraction.

It was her vulnerability: this tortured beautiful woman caught in the unhappy marriage – although he'd experienced that before, and never felt sympathetic. But as cavalier as he wanted to be, he identified there was something new here. It might just be a speck, but that was a speck more than anything else he'd ever experienced.

"You ever read any of his books?" he asked.

"I've read them all," Milo said. "There're only three – well, he's at this book signing for his fourth."

"Why didn't you tell me?"

"Shockingly, the topic never got around to books I'd read by husbands of women you're fucking. Until now, that is."

Jake smirked.

"I'll loan you one of his books. Have a read for yourself."

"What good's that going to do?"

"You can tell a lot about these guys by the way they write – their ideas and that. And I think you'll like it."

"Why?"

Milo grinned. "You like his wife."

"Very funny."

Milo lifted his beer and toasted Jake's glass, sitting unattended on the table. "To the stupid fucking things your cock gets you into."

"It'll be fine."

"Your cock or the situation?"

"*Both.*"

"I hope so, Jake. For your sake."

28.

Skip toyed with his ravioli, nimbly spun his fork in his hand – he'd learned to twirl a pen in between his fingers in high school because he thought it'd impress people – then prodded at his ravioli again. Sherry lifted her ice water with an abruptness that showed her annoyance. He guzzled down his beer, then fetched a fresh Singha out of the fridge. Sherry sighed like she didn't want him to hear, but actually did. They ate, their cutlery on porcelain like clanging symbols.

She took her plate over to the sink, trying to mask that she wasn't moving fluidly. He'd seen her like this once before – after a high-impact aerobics class. But she wasn't exercising now. This was probably from high-impact fucking. He wrote such scenes – unfortunately, they weren't from experience, unless frequenting porn sites counted.

What sort of man was he? Another author? Luis? Skip almost laughed out loud. He remembered overhearing the tone of Sherry's playfulness when she'd been in the tub. No way she was having those sorts of conversations with Luis. Skip had heard stories about Luis that involved bondage and sadomasochism. Sherry would never subject herself to that. Maybe it was somebody not so cerebral this time. The guy at the bar! *Really cute* – that's how she'd described him. That's when this had started – the night her car had broken down. It was a leap, but leaps got stories underway.

"I might take a bath," she said.

While she was in the tub, he rifled through her purse and found her phone. He searched the messages – the only inexplicable message was a blank text she'd sent herself. Skip checked the date and time – the other night, when she'd claimed Luis had messaged her about more changes. So here was proof she'd faked that. He checked her phone log, but that seemed fine. Of course, it was easy enough to delete records of incriminating calls. He put her phone away.

Grabbing himself another beer, he chomped on three Xanax, thinking he wouldn't be able to write, but he gradually lost himself in his story until he was chasing the narrative on the page. He wrote until midnight, went to bed, and found Sherry asleep. How long did they last like this? He should've done the dinner. And the restaurant. All of it. Although it would've meant nothing. She was involved – not thinking about it, but *involved*. He was sure of that now. The anxiousness exploded. This is it how it had been at school – always losing out, and powerless to stop it. It didn't matter who he became, and the image he strove to maintain, because he always remained who he was.

He slept poorly, Sherry's call from downstairs waking him early morning: "Skip, Tyson's here!" He blinked into sunlight blazing through the windows, the curtains luminous and the ceiling aglow. The world hadn't stopped. He kept waking to these mornings. Everybody did. He imagined an array of faces in an array of rooms rising in an array of beds. They got up, confronted their problems, and – for good or bad – tried to live their lives.

The only alternative was surrender, which held its own allure – to not worry about any of this shit.

He hauled himself out of bed and pulled on some clothes.

Tyson waited in the foyer, an iPad in hand. Skip heard Sherry's car start and reverse onto the street.

"Did you confront her?" Tyson asked.

Skip shook his head. "What've you got?"

"We should get you some coffee."

Skip led Tyson into the kitchen, grabbed himself a beer, and downed a Xanax.

"Did you get my order?"

Tyson plucked another bottle from his pocket and placed it on the table. "Skip—"

"Get on with the rest."

"Skip—?"

"Now, Tyson."

Tyson put his iPad down next to the bottle. "The agency retains a private investigator on the odd occasion - you know, look into claims of plagiarism, that sort of thing."

"You had him follow Sherry?"

"*Her*. And yes. Before I show you these, I want you to brace—"

"Show me."

"I—"

"Show me, Tyson."

"They're distress—"

"*Show. Me.*"

Tyson swiped the iPad, keyed in his code, and brought up the gallery. The pictures were from up high and framed through a second-story window. The first was of Sherry and a sandy-haired athletic guy - a cliché, if you were going to write that sort - kissing. The shots grew progressively riskier: Sherry going down on him; him between her legs; various positions on bed; several leaning against the bed, or walls, or the windowpane. Then it wasn't just risky, but adventurous. Skip had seen such couplings on porn sites, but had always believed they were just poses. Nope. Here was evidence people really did those things if they were capable.

He flicked through the shots and extrapolated a history – guy was popular in high school, probably good at sports but never good enough to make a career of it; he bummed around in bars, enjoying the recreation of the job and the opportunity to fuck women (and men), before getting his own place. Life came so breezily to him. He didn't care about repercussions. Guys like him never did. The world just remolded around them – or so they thought.

"I know this is a shock," Tyson said, "but, well, it's not unexpected. Remember, she started seeing you *before* she dumped me."

"True to form, huh?"

"She was dating an editor at Token Publishing when she started seeing me!"

Skip looked at the way the guy was wedged between Sherry's legs, her legs splayed wide, ankles dangling above her shoulders, her back arched, face (even as blurry as it was in the shots) contorted in a pleasure he'd seen often enough, but never with such abandon. He'd always thought

Sherry the sophisticate, although her background was middle-class – her parents had divorced, then both long-term remarried other partners. The truth was that, whatever the preconception, being sophisticated didn't make her *reserved*. Or conservative. Here he saw her unbound and free ... although he had a faint recollection she'd been some semblance of this early in their relationship.

He gulped down his beer and grabbed another from the fridge. "Let yourself out, Tyson."

"Skip—?"

"Go! Now!"

"Skip, I don't—"

Skip shoved him in the chest. Tyson stumbled back and held up his hands. Skip herded him down the hallway.

"Skip, I've been through this! I can hel—"

Skip yanked open the door and jostled Tyson out. Tyson tripped on the doorstep and almost plummeted down the veranda steps. He caught the balustrade, teetered, then righted himself, his face contorting in some bizarre expression, half his mouth twisting, his opposing eye squinting, but his forehead remaining ridiculously unfurrowed – maybe it was a grimace. But then everything smoothed out, like a wrinkled handkerchief that had been ironed.

Tyson held up a finger, like he was going to make a point. "Now, Skip—"

Skip slammed the door and thumped through the house, picking up one of the Waterford Crystal vases and wanting to smash it. He hoisted it above his head. Stopped. The vase had done nothing. This was about him. And Sherry. He was still the unpopular guy losing out. She was one of the cool kids whose actions mocked him. He'd show her then. He'd show them all.

He put the vase back and went to the kitchen.

The bottle of Xanax Tyson had brought waited on the kitchen table. There was no reluctance, no regret. Skip moved with the certainty that his life had been pointed at this moment. Of all the things he'd created, this would be his most spectacular endeavor yet.

He opened the bottle and upended the pills into his mouth – and then did the same with his other bottle. He washed them down with beer, then stumbled from the kitchen, and made his way outside.

He jumped into the pool and floated onto his back.

And waited for the inevitable to take him.

29.

Editors poured studiously through manuscripts, while designers whipped up covers or worked on book layouts. The publicist, and members of her team, were abuzz, chasing up marketing opportunities on their phones, or hammering away at social media or emails. Sherry even saw Ben, the intern, peek shyly at her from behind a computer. To most, it might've seemed disorganized, if not random, but Sherry recognized the synchronicity.

At times like this, she missed working on-site, regardless of the office's lack of personality – this collective creativity transcended it and networked everybody into a hive mind that harmonized into a singular vision (or, to be more precise, a collection of singular visions), implicit with the hope that in a world without magic, they were creating something magical.

She reached Pria's office and knocked on the door jamb. Pria, as composed and radiant as ever, looked up from a hardcopy manuscript – as much as editing was done onscreen nowadays, Pria always preferred hardcopies. She said she saw *more*. She was right. But this was why she was such a brilliant editor – Gray's had always known it. They'd kept her out of managerial for as long as they could.

"I need somebody to talk to." Sherry said.

"Come in. Close the door."

Sherry did that and sat on the chair opposite Pria.

"I don't know where to begin."

"Remember what I taught you," Pria said. "Take a breath. Think. Focus. Articulate."

Sherry did just that. Everything was a pulse in her head: the guilt, the attraction to Jake, the conflict, the confusion about her feelings for Jake versus what she felt now for Skip, the excitement about the future, the lament about what the present had become – there was so much to contend with.

If it had been a story, she could prioritize importance based on what the narrative needed. But fiction had to make sense. Readers were discerning. They would flag contrivances and stupidities and improbabilities. Things couldn't happen without justification. Readers got tangled up in the knots of bad plotting.

Pria opened her desk drawer, and plucked out two glasses, and a small flask. "I allow myself the odd libation." She filled each glass with a shot of clear liquid from the flask. "I know it's not healthy, and I know it's early, but sometimes you just need to do what you need to do to get by."

Sherry sipped from the glass, then downed it in one gulp – gin. It didn't help.

"You're the best editor I've ever known," Pria said, refilling her glass. "You cannot teach that understanding of story and structure, only develop and hone it. I've imparted all my wisdom, but the truth is before we even met, you were already a better editor than me."

"Thank you," Sherry said – this was not praise she'd heard before, but it meant nothing right now.

"So it's doubtful this is a professional matter," Pria said. "Personal, then. Skip, of course. Skip is as brilliant as he is stupid."

Sherry almost spluttered out her gin.

"I've learned a thing or two in my thirty years in the industry. An ex of mine long, long, long ago coined the term *whorethurs*: those who aspire to the romanticism of being a writer and sell out to the image; then you have those who do whatever they need to do. Finally, there are those *savants* who exist only to create, to tell stories. They can write about the dynamics of relationships with divine understanding, insight, and empathy, yet don't know how to interact with people. Skip is a savant – charming, charismatic, and even more brilliant than he realizes, but a savant all the same."

"Maybe that's what I fell in love with," Sherry said.

"Have you met somebody else?"

Sherry stiffened.

"You come in, beaming one day, and a mess another. You were beaming because you met somebody who makes you feel desired."

"Skip makes me feel like an appendage."

"And this other relationship? How far has it developed?"

Sherry's grip on her glass tightened.

"Is it serious or a fling?"

"I … don't … know."

"You're caught in the nexus where emotions rage. Be discreet. You're a professional woman. A professional woman does not need a scandal. You've always been impulsive in love. Skip, Tyson, Ethan – before Ethan it was that man with the bike, Rodney? And before him that artist who would sketch you, Marcus. And before that—"

"I get the idea," Sherry said, reeling – she'd forgotten some of those names.

"Impetuosity can be romantic," Pria said. "But it can also be a façade – a glamorous shopfront with nothing inside but gaudy décor and yesterday's fashions."

"What are you trying to tell me?"

"Do you like to fuck this man?"

Sherry almost laughed – Pria's prim accent glamorized the profanity.

"Well?" Pria arched one finely plucked brow.

"The sex is so combative."

"Is that a good thing?"

"I lose myself in it. I did that with Skip intellectually. We'd argue about his writing. We found something in that. This is the same on a physical level. I've never felt that way before."

"Beyond that?"

Sherry didn't know. And it was obvious Jake didn't.

"Let me offer you a warning," Pria said. "You don't need distractions right now – not with the upheaval about to take place here. Who knows? Perhaps you'll find this is simply a firework – dazzling initially, but when it's gone, what are you left with? Nothing but night. And Skip."

"Whatever else happens," Sherry said, and now the words did come, slow and clumsy, but she felt them to be true, "I think Skip and I have gone as far as we can go. There was no great demise. It just fizzled away. It feels like we're together because that's the habit we've established."

"Many relationships *are* habits – they are the worst kind. Wake up, address the day's routine, sleep, and do it all over. They are so dazzlingly mundane they lack the conflict, those explosive confrontations, that would otherwise highlight issues, signposts, that suggest the relationship not only *should* come to an end, but *needs to*. It's only years later that reflection delineates how unfulfilling habit can be."

"Then what do I do?"

"In a little over three months, I mark my twenty-fifth wedding anniversary." Pria span a silver picture frame on her desk to reveal her and her husband, a distinguished man in a charcoal suit that fit him so neatly, it had to be tailor-made. "Graham is a delight. He makes me breakfast in bed every Sunday. He is intelligent and funny. He understands my countless overtime and has never once criticized me about it. He is a lawyer and a partner in his firm. His good qualities are overwhelming. But he can be a pain. He's perfunctory when he washes the dishes. He insists on leaving the toilet door open when he does his business. And he's horrible at keeping track of his spending. A relationship is a myriad of extremes – you can never have just one side of things. But the good *should* outweigh the bad."

"After twenty-five years, are you still happy?"

"Sometimes I need the pain to appreciate the delight, and you do things to keep the relationship alive. As far as this other man goes, what does he feel about you? Or does he exist as a device to pry you from Skip because that's what you need? Sometimes, we act thinking we're being true to ourselves, to our conscious needs when, in truth," she tapped her temple, "we're serving some need festering deep inside us and which we're not ready to face." She sipped from her gin. "Well? Do you know what the case is as far as you're concerned?"

Sherry didn't have an answer for that.

"This is *what* you need to work out," Pria said.

30.

Jake sat on a stool at the bar and flipped to the next page of *Midday, Midnight, Dawn*, his eyes following the narrative with the mindless glee of a ball bouncing over karaoke lyrics. Skip Lago's prose was simple, the story engaging, the world immersive. The book itself was a fucker over five hundred pages, so Jake was surprised at how quickly he was mowing through it.

The door jangled open – Sherry, delectable in a pair of faded jeans and a peach blouse. It was like she'd dressed down, which only delineated just how aristocratic she was – a socialite slumming it. But then he polarized his interpretation: he was despoiling a classy woman, corrupting her with his vices.

She surveyed the bar. Only a handful of the tables were occupied.

"Quiet," she said.

"Gets busier as the day goes on. I didn't expect to see you."

"Disappointed?"

Jake rested the opened book face down on the bar. The plan was to come around the bar and wrap Sherry in a hug and kiss her because he was genuinely happy to see her. But her gaze went straight to the novel – of course it would.

"Is that …?" Sherry placed her hand on the cover. "Why the hell are you reading this?"

"It's … you know?"

Sherry apparently didn't; she glowered at him in a way that made him feel like a kid getting into trouble.

"You talk about your husband and, well, I wanted to get a sense of him."

"Why should you even care? I asked you to think about this – *us*. Not *him*."

"What do you want from me?"

"More than I'm getting. Something tangible."

Real. Tangible. He'd already seen the signs but had been dismissive. She wanted to get serious. And maybe she had a right to. No, she definitely did – that's what Milo had been warning him about. But these were demands for which Jake was unprepared. He liked her. He loved fucking her. He'd love to feel her lips around his cock right now. The bonus was that would put an end to this conversation.

Sherry waited, folding her arms across her chest.

"Why do you need this all right now?" Jake said. "It's like this has just accelerated from go to woe."

"So, I'm 'woe' – is that it?"

"I didn't mean it that way," Jake said.

"Then what am I?" she said. "Just a fuck?"

Jake's eyes darted nervously around the bar. The few patrons were watching them.

"I didn't say that," he said.

"Given your reaction—"

"This is going too quickly."

Sherry clenched her jaw. "How quickly do you usually move, Jake?"

"Sherry—"

She charged out.

Jake hurdled the bar, bolted out, and was chasing Sherry across the parking lot even before he realized he was doing it. It hadn't been so long ago that he'd been able to play it cool, but now he found himself skittering to a halt right in front of her car, ready to slam his palms down onto the hood and cry out her name. That would've been the uncharacteristic response – so uncharacteristic that it froze him mid-action. This was not him. This had *never* been him. And he was not making a grand gesture for a woman he'd just met. He didn't want to lose her but wasn't going all in because her expectations were on a timetable different to his.

She started the car, revved the engine, and, when he didn't move, reversed. The tires screeched on the asphalt. She revved the engine again. He rose, folding his arms across his chest like he was daring her. She accelerated but swerved around him, glowering at him as she passed. He was unflinching. She'd learn, even if he had to fuck it into her. And she would be back. She was the one burning her ties – not him.

He returned to The Rap, opening the door to the sight of a redhead leaning on the bar, calling out, "Hello!" Three attractive, twenty-something women sat at one of the nearby tables. They must've come in while he'd been chasing Sherry. He welcomed the distraction.

"Sorry!" he said. "Just had to see somebody out. What can I get you?"

"It's okay—" the redhead began, turning.

Her mouth dropped open in such a comical overstated way that Jake would've laughed if she wasn't so familiar – it was the freckles that did it: she was the woman he'd picked up at The Back Room, and who he'd fucked in the alley. The three women at the table were her friends. He recognized the adversarial one with the square jaw.

"You work here?" Freckles asked.

Jake couldn't remember what he'd told her.

"You told me you were a physio."

"I do part-time here."

"What was your name again?" Square Jaw said. "Teddy?"

Everybody was glaring at him – even the other patrons. He didn't like the attention. They'd just witnessed his altercation with Sherry, and now this. Two of Freckles' friends came around to flank her, like they were planning to fight him. Square Jaw drew up by his side. He was cornered – the only way out was back through the door.

"Well?" Square Jaw said.

She was testing him. He'd never use an alias like Teddy – although he couldn't recall if he *had* used an alias. He did, sometimes, when he was feeling mischievous, or he'd recite the wrong phone number, transposing the last two digits (just in case they somehow found him, he could claim they'd taken it down wrong). But he couldn't remember which he'd done, or if he'd done either at all. Given the volume of women he'd fucked, these things had grown hard to keep track of.

"Jake," he said.

Freckles burst into tears.

"You told her your name was 'Jimmy'!" Square Jaw said.

Trapped. Stupidly. Funnily, "Jimmy" didn't seem the sort of alias he'd use either.

"People call me Jimmy," he said. "It's Jake James Rappa—"

"You ... fucking ... liar," Freckles sobbed. "You know I broke up with my fiancé because of you? Because of how guilty I felt?"

She was standing right before him now, nostrils flaring, green eyes so bright and incendiary that her wrath might've been something divine. He'd had women this angry at him before. They were easy to manipulate because there was so much to work with. He'd even fucked a few – a goodbye fuck. The problem here was the friends. He wasn't going to win them over – especially Square Jaw.

"You took advantage of me!" Freckles said.

He had no way of defusing this. It was done. He could be contrite, or brave through it. That was the best choice. He might've seduced her, but she *was* willing, and she had to take responsibility for that.

"I sold the lies," he said. "I didn't force you to buy them."

Freckles slapped him – a good slap, too, that rocked his head. Jake absorbed it, then stood unmoving. She charged out, the two friends chasing after her. Square Jaw hovered around to face Jake, and she wasn't priming for a slap. He could see her right-hand clenching. This woman would try and punch him out.

"You're a cunt," she said.

She lifted her arm, moving with a competence that suggested she probably trained in some discipline – kickboxing or Muay Thai or something. He braced himself; he'd give her a shot. But as if realizing resorting to violence might offer him some sort of moral victory – that he'd incited her to such action – she lowered her arm and shook her head once.

Then she was out the door.

31.

Floating in the pool, squinting into the blaring sun, Skip visualized his funeral: it would be overcast, with the occasional rumble of thunder threatening to escalate into a storm. A choir would open with Mozart's Requiem Mass. The marble headstone would bear his full name – the one Tyson said sounded like a market fishmonger: *Scipio Camberlago*. A demure Sherry, guilt-ridden and resplendent in black, a veil hanging low over her face, would lead rows and rows and rows of inconsolably sobbing mourners.

No. This was all too pretentious.

Backstep: it'd be a beautiful day, the weeping willows casting long shadows across the cemetery. A bearded priest would stand over his plot. The headstone would still be the same. On one side would be Sherry, sobbing (and the sobbing would still be guilt-ridden), knowing her betrayal had driven him to this. Opposite her, exulting with moral superiority, yet distraught, and also secretly delighting that death would popularize sales, would be Tyson. Maybe a scattering of authors would attend. Well, maybe just Luis, in mismatched clothes, drinking from a bottle in a brown paper bag. And some of the higher-ups from Gray's, although their presence was observing a formality, rather than a friendship. There would be no friends. And no family.

It was pathetic – a horrible way to go out. He'd impacted nobody on a personal level. Well, except for Sherry. And she no longer counted. He should've had at least one real friend. That would be good – somebody who could remember him on that personal level for *who* he was.

They *would* remember him on a professional level. His writing *had* touched readers. He was good at it – or, at least, competent. Writing was the only time he fit. He didn't fit with Sherry – not really. He loved her … and then, he wasn't sure if that was true either.

He loved the idea of being in love, in having somebody who believed in him and inspired him and supported him, but he and Sherry didn't share any great connection. Or *any* connection, except when they talked about writing – well, about *his* writing since their literary tastes differed. But she *was* brilliant, a guru herself in understanding story, being true to his narrative voice, and always knowing how to coax the best out of him. That was it, though. He couldn't place any other genuine conversation he had with her. She was the jewel on the image he'd built for himself.

And dying, he found he wouldn't miss her. He *would* miss the writing – especially now it was going so well. Avenues were opening up. This was the truest thing about his existence. This is where he succeeded when everything else was either failing or a pretense. And this is why he didn't have friends (although now, in retrospect, he thought he should have at least one): writing was the priority in his life. Why was he leaving it? Was he even leaving it?

Skip's arms and legs were growing sore from being held out to float, his face tingling from roasting in the sun (he considered how red-faced his corpse would be, like he'd been ashamed about taking his own life), and he needed to pee. How long had he been in the pool? An hour? More? He'd swallowed over seventy Xanax. They should've started taking effect within five minutes.

He let his legs sink into the water, and his feet touch the pool floor. He lifted one hand, and then the other.

Xanax came with a euphoric peacefulness, as well as a heaviness about the limbs. He hadn't felt either for years – he'd believed that was because his habit kept him permanently in that state so it'd had become so normalized he could no longer distinguish it from any other waking moment. But if this overdose hadn't worked, that meant it was likely the pills hadn't worked either for years, or he'd been kidding himself.

Kidding himself seemed the likelier option – especially given he chased the Xanaxes down with beer, beer, and more beer. They would've disguised the lack of any effects like heavy limbs or drowsiness and would've discouraged him from being too self-analytical.

Tyson! At some point, he must've swapped out the Xanax for placebos. Skip couldn't work out when it had happened – probably when one of his heavier drinking periods could entirely mask the switch, although he ruefully reflected that provided a lot of opportunities.

Skip swam to the pool's edge, then climbed out. He took off his shirt and went back into the house. He left his t-shirt in the foyer, his pants on the stairs, his underwear on the landing, one sock in his bedroom, and then his other in the bathroom.

He stared at himself in the mirror – his wet hair, his scraggly beard, and his sunburned face.

He opened the bathroom cabinet.

32.

Sherry couldn't drive home. She couldn't face Skip, couldn't face that big house, couldn't face a life that was growing increasingly redundant. She didn't want anything but her own company, so she drove into the city and circled the block again and again, a mindless crawl that became meditative in its inanity, and gave her time and space to think.

Jake disturbingly occupied too many of her thoughts. She hadn't known what she'd expected from him – maybe a sign that this wasn't just all whim, as Pria had suggested. It couldn't just be lust. She couldn't be giving herself for nothing. It kept coming back to this. He *had* to feel more – just like Skip had when they'd begun dating even though she was meant to be attached to Tyson.

She saw parking on the street and took it, intending to window shop as she thought things through, but found a bar, Hopman's, a dim railway carriage whose highlight was the bookshelf that lined the entire length of the rear wall.

There were classics from authors such as F. Scott Fitzgerald, Jane Austen, and Charles Dickens, as well as contemporary authors like Michael Crichton, Stephen King, and Liane Moriarty, and there was a Skip Lago, and a Luis Stauss, as well as some of her other authors. Sherry sunk onto a stool at the bar. This was her contribution to the literary community. Skip and Luis would go on and have prestigious careers – Skip a commercial behemoth, Luis a literary paragon. And who would know her, an anonymous editor?

"What'll it be?"

The bartender was young, athletic, and had the forearms and chest of somebody who worked out lots, but hadn't yet escaped his adolescent baby fat. His dark hair was slicked back with some greasy product. His eyes unashamedly roved her body. Because that's what men did when they met her, immediately contemplating how they could win her. She'd always known it and accepted it, but now it angered her.

"A beer's fine," she said.

"What sort?"

"Whatever's on tap."

The bartender poured her a beer; she slid a twenty across the bar and told him to keep the change. He smiled and thanked her, then began stacking empties into the sink – although he kept glancing back at her. She could hear his mind whir, trying to concoct conversation openers. He knew she was out of his league, but it didn't stop him aspiring.

"You come in here before?" he said.

"No."

Sherry pictured herself fucking him, riding him while his fingers dug into her buttocks. She shifted on the stool. He would be so easy to have. Men just were. Skip had been as moralistic as she'd encountered, although it was likelier his tentativeness had to do with his awkwardness and inexperience.

The bartender came over. His face was even more boyish up close, and he still had faint acne on his chin. He might've been eighteen or nineteen, although he had a slyness that suggested a confidence that came from experience. He was good looking enough to have capitalized through high school and landed older women if he went to bars and clubs. He was Jake Jr.

"Want to say something to me?" Sherry said.

He planted his hands on the bar so his biceps flexed. He opened his mouth.

"Or maybe you want to fuck?" Sherry said.

His mouth froze in an O.

"Or I could come behind the bar and blow you."

The tent in his crotch bulged. Sherry got up from her stool and smiled.

"Take it out," she told him.

"What?"

"You don't hear so well?"

"You want me to—"

"Take it out," Sherry told him.

"Are you seri—?"

"I am. Are you?"

He smirked as that same confidence lit up his face. No sane person would do what she said, but aroused, immature men were far from sane. They lost all rationality, their reason malleable – a beautiful stranger spontaneously propositioning them for impromptu sex? Sure, why not? Why wouldn't such a thing happen?

Unbuttoning his jeans, he unzipped them, and eased out his cock as if he were handling a priceless relic that he was reluctant to pass over. He was circumcised, and big. His pubic hair had been trimmed. Sherry realized he wasn't reluctant. This was all a show – he'd perfected an unveiling act to impress, like a magician revealing the prestige of a trick to wow an audience.

"What do you think?" he said.

It was this easy. But now Sherry saw a pivotal flaw in her relationships. She gave herself to partners. That's why Skip could take her for granted, and Jake could use her for sex. She should've been asking them to give themselves to her before she committed herself to any great love affair.

"Well?" the bartender said.

Sherry lifted her beer like she was going to take a drink as she mulled over what came next, then thrust the glass forward, splashing the beer all over his cock.

"Hey!" The bartender leaped back, scrambling for a towel. "You bitch!"

Sherry hurled the glass at him. He swayed back instinctively. The glass hit a row of bottles behind him, shattering them.

"You fucking tiny, little boy," she said.

She strode away from the bar, but by the time she reached the door she was swaggering. His incomprehensible swearing chased her all the way back to the car. She drove home, rediscovering not only a sense of equilibrium, but ownership over her life. A musky evening, sticky with the warmth of the day, was settling over the house when she pulled into the drive next to Skip's Mustang.

On the veranda by the front door was a plush, vibrating recliner – well, that was Skip, buying things impulsively. She went inside. His study door was mostly closed. Some Mozart opera she couldn't identify (but guessed might be "Cosi fan tutte") blared. His fingers were raindrops on the keyboard. She reached for the door, then stopped.

He was writing. How would he respond to hearing about her affair? It'd destroy his writing. She hated that because she did genuinely value that side of him – he was nothing without his writing. Her heart thudded. She hadn't felt this wariness with Tyson. Was that respect for Skip? Or respect for his writing? Or just indifference to Tyson, who was a mercenary professionally, but vacuous personally?

She charged up the stairs and darted into her bedroom to pack an overnight bag and some toiletries. Skip would be hurt, but that was life. He'd recover. It was a rationalization, but also life. Relationships were always breaking up. And he deserved to know as soon as possible. She couldn't put it off. Bag packed, she went back downstairs.

The study was quiet now. She swung the door open. Empty. A car roared outside. She hurried to the front door – Skip was pulling out of the drive. Rushing out to the veranda, she waved, trying to signal him to stop. Surely he had to see her. But he reversed from the house, then drove off.

As she made her way back to her car, she took out her phone, and brought up Skip's phone number. She rang, but it went through to voicemail. Getting in her car, she tried again, but got the same result.

Dumping her phone in the change compartment, she started her car, then looked up.

And froze.

Scrawled on the outside of the windscreen in lipstick, but written mirror-image so she could read it from inside the car was a single word:

Cheater

To Sherry's surprise, what she experienced then wasn't dread, or guilt, but relief. He knew. She didn't know how (but figured it somehow featured Tyson) but Skip knew and that was that.

She could move on.

33.

As they walked from The Rap to Blaise's Bookstore, Jake's tension simmered into a gnawing unease that reminded him of the way he'd felt waiting for the prognosis on the knee injury that had derailed his football career.

"I'm surprised you agreed to this," Milo said.

"I thought you might have a point," Jake said.

But it was less about Milo's nagging and more about Freckles' appearance. Jake had endured outbursts before, weathered them, and then dismissed them. Everybody was responsible for their own actions, as well as the repercussions. This was different. Perhaps it was a combination of Freckles' earnestness, Milo's nagging, and Sherry's probing. Whatever the case, Jake didn't like it, and wanted to find a way to put it back into a context he could understand.

Blaise's Bookstore was just a fifteen-minute walk from The Rap, sitting on the city's outskirts among a collection of old boutique stores and quaint cafes. A line of people extended from the entrance and down the street. Jake thought there'd be a type – geeks, mostly, like Milo – who preferred to stick their nose in a book rather than go to a club or a show or go out and hook up. But there were all sorts: young, old, attractive, unattractive, people with partners, people who were single – there had to be something to this writing shtick.

Jake and Milo took their position at the end of the queue. Others fell in behind them.

"How much of that book did you read?" Milo asked.

"All of it."

"Whoa. Amazing."

"When we used to read those classics in school, I didn't understand a single word. This was simple.

And I like the story was about something normal going really fucked-up wrong."

"I thought that might appeal to you."

As the line moved, Jake studied the people who dribbled from Blaise's Bookstore, grasping purchases to their chests. He caught snippets as they passed, things like "he's so funny" and "he smiled at me" and "I can't believe what he signed!" How could a cuckold inspire such awe?

Blaise's Bookstore was big but orderly: a broad aisle dissected rows and rows of shelves, along with a stairwell – right next to a little café section – spiraling up to a second floor. By the counter, a pyramid of *Cold Enterprises* greeted them. Milo grabbed two, although from around the base, easing them out so the rest didn't capsize. He thrust one into Jake's midriff.

"What's this for?" he said.

"What do you think he's going to sign? Your cock?"

The line continued to move. Jake teetered left and right, trying to see the table it led to – and Skip sitting there – but too many people were in the way.

"Have you contemplated what you want from this relationship?" Milo said.

"We fuck. It's fun."

"You keep seeing her. This tells you something, doesn't it?"

"Like what?"

Milo snorted. "Are you serious?"

"Why do we keep coming back to this?"

"Because you drift, Jake. You drifted through school, drifted through a football career—"

"I did not."

"Jake, you were so fucking good, but you tried to get by on talent alone. Then, when you did your knee, you drifted through rehab."

"It was a career-ending injury. What did you want me to do?"

"Some people would've tried regardless."

"It was pointless."

"Okay, fine. So then you became a bartender and drifted from bar to bar. The Rap was the first time you chased something. I loved that you did that - you saw something, you focused, you went and made it happen. I think you need that in other aspects of your life."

"Not everybody has it worked out like you."

"I didn't have it worked out," Milo said. "You *know* I had no idea what I was doing coming out of high school. The difference is I committed to things."

"Like Alice. Well done that some woman—"

"You want to be careful about what you say next, Jake."

"I've always teased you about marriage."

"But not about Alice. Not about her personally. Do *not* disrespect her."

Milo's flat hostility surprised Jake – it was something he had *never* seen in twenty years of friendship. He'd seen Milo angry; he'd seen Milo scrap in high school when kids had picked on him because he'd always been a little short, a little plump, a little clumsy – Jake had rescued him repeatedly in fights. But this was something different – Jake reluctantly conceded that it came from pride Milo felt over the woman he'd married, the kids he'd fathered, and the life he continued to build, and decided that was fair enough.

"Okay, okay," Jake said, "I'm sorry. I didn't mean anything by about it. But you keep going on about relationships. Married people always want to marry off their friends."

"This one's obviously having an effect on you."

"So?"

"Maybe she'd be good for you."

"Who'd be good for you?"

The question came from Skip Lago. They were now at the front of the table. He didn't resemble the picture Blaise's had up on their website – his head had been shaved close, and his face was a sunburnt pink. His shadowy growth was neatly trimmed, his eyes a muddy olive. So, this was Mr. Bigshot Author – a scraggly overgrown baby with sunburn or diaper rash or something.

"Just relationship stuff," Milo said. He thrust his copy of *Cold Enterprise* at Skip. "Make it out to Milo. *To your best friend Milo*, actually."

Skip chuckled, opened the book, and signed the title page.

"Is it true this one's going to be a flick?" Milo asked.

Skip held out the book to Milo. "There's talk."

"You writing it?" Milo took his book. "If anybody could adapt it, I'm sure you could."

"But ...?"

"How do you condense five hundred pages into two hours of movie-time, especially with the shoddy filmmakers out there?"

"I should get you to be my agent."

Milo clutched *Cold Enterprise* to his chest. "I take fifteen per cent."

"Sounds about right."

"How long until your next book comes out?"

"I'm working on it."

Skip gestured for Jake's book. Jake planned to flick it to him, like he was skipping a rock across a lake, but he fumbled it, and the book splattered unceremoniously on the table. Skip flinched briefly, picked up the book carefully like it might be broken and he wanted to make sure it wouldn't fragment, all while he held Jake's gaze, as if trying to place him. Every muscle in Jake's body coiled. That wasn't the casual examination of somebody checking out a stranger for the first time; there was a familiarity there, if not an identification. Then it hit Jake: *Skip knew!* Jake wasn't sure how, but the little pink prick knew.

"Who should I make it out to?" Skip asked.

"J–J–Jake."

"J–J–Jake it is."

As Skip began to write on the title page, Jake took a deep breath and drew himself up. He didn't have to be nervous – he didn't know why that had even entered the equation. If Skip knew, good. *Great.* Fuck him. He should know how he made Sherry scream with orgasm, how he'd taken her every way he could, how she supplicated herself as if in cock worship. She wouldn't be doing any of that if she were getting anything worthwhile from this fucktard. And obviously he *was* a fucktard. What other man would just sit there, knowing he was facing his wife's lover, and do nothing about it?

"So, is this satisfying?" Jake asked.

"What?" Skip asked.

"Writing. You know: geek stuff."

"I like it."

"Seems nerdy to me."

Skip chuckled. "Feel like I'm back in high school."

He voice wasn't the high-pitched stereotype of some movie nerd, but deep and just the littlest bit gravelly, although it wavered minutely – the cuckold was nervous. For as much as he was a bigshot, certain dynamics didn't change. He was a geek putting on a face, and Jake's presence had cracked that. He was tempted to shatter it entirely.

"Just curious what makes somebody write," he said. "Feels like endless English homework."

"What makes anybody do anything?" Skip asked.

He tried to whip the book closed, scoop it up, and thrust it out to Jake, but it slipped from his hands and skittered across the table. Milo leaned in reflexively, like he was going to catch it, but Jake held out an arm to keep him it at bay. Skip *did* grab it, both hands shooting out awkwardly – the hand holding the pen accidentally scribbling a line across the tablecloth; with the other, he seized up the book, unwittingly bending the top corner of the cover.

And then he held it there, a meek offering from a peasant to his lord.

Jake didn't take it – not immediately. He was sure Skip's hand shook. The unease between them thickened. The only thing that bored through it was the gaze Milo directed at Jake; Jake could *feel* it, but he did not avert his attention from Skip.

"You rich?" Jake asked.

"Not really. Not yet."

"You nerds," Jake said, finally taking the book, "you never change, huh?"

"Guess not." Skip leaned back in his chair, as if to gain distance from him.

Jake wanted to obliterate him then – truly obliterate him, although he didn't know what form that would take, or why such anger should exist outside of the resentment that this guy was married to Sherry. But that was stupid; this guy might be married to Sherry, but Jake was the one fucking her.

Milo pressed a hand into the small of his back. "We should be going," he said. "Thanks."

Jake allowed himself to be steered away, but only because he exulted in the moral triumph. What he really wanted now more than anything was Sherry, like she was a prize to be claimed and despoiled. But he doubted he could tell her about this episode. If she'd gotten *that* upset finding him reading one of Skip's books, telling her about the signing would be a definite no-go zone.

Milo led them to the cashier, where he paid for the books. They drifted out onto the street. The queue to see Skip wasn't getting any shorter. They might've been villagers worshipping a false god. Jake cocked his arm back, ready to fling his book into traffic and demolish their reverence. Milo caught him by the wrist.

"Hey!"

Jake lowered his arm.

"What the fuck was that?" Milo said. "You want to bully him like you're in high school?"

"Fuck him."

"What happened back there, that was just … just fucking embarrassing."

"You wanted me to meet him," Jake said. "He's a nobody. In fact, seeing the loser he is, no wonder his wife's cheating. Why wouldn't she?"

"You're having sex with his wife, and you're treating him like he's wronged you."

"It's just that—"

"I don't care what comes next, Jake."

"But—"

"Just shut it, okay?"

They fell into an uneasy quiet that Jake didn't enjoy. Milo reproached him – *genuinely* reproached him – rarely, and when he did it was deserved. Jake would usually concede graciously. He'd pushed this way too far. However Jake felt about Skip, Milo didn't deserve this, but Jake wasn't sure how to broach it. They didn't speak another word until they reached The Rap's front door.

"I should get back to work," Milo said.

"I pissed you off, huh?" Jake asked.

"Jake, I love you, but … seriously? All those one-nighters. Fine. There and done. All those meaningless flings? Okay. But this is serious now. And, well … just grow the fuck up, man." Milo sighed. "This isn't just about you. When do you realize that?"

Jake didn't have an answer, but Milo was right. Freckles had proven that.

"I'll see you later."

Jake had felt Milo's disappointment before, but never so deeply. This wasn't just a dismissible disagreement, but in thinking that Jake realized they'd never been dismissible. He'd disregarded Milo's concerns, and Milo hadn't pushed it – had *never* pushed it out of courtesy. This was the culmination of all those occasions.

Shaken, Jake went back into The Rap. Karen was vigorously polishing the bar, her breasts bouncing in a thin t-shirt that revealed too much cleavage. It was the sort of observation Jake would've made countless times before, but now he noticed how it was the first thing his attention went to.

"Hey, boss," Karen said, without looking up from her work, "your girlfriend's upstairs."

His *girlfriend*.

Jake smiled, determined to find delight in that: his *girlfriend*. And that also provided him the answer: he was antagonistic toward Skip because he was Sherry's husband. Jake didn't like that. He'd had plenty of sex with women who'd had other partners, but he was growing territorial about Sherry. Maybe Milo had a point, and as puerile as Jake's own conceptualization of relationships was, maybe this was a new beginning.

"Thanks," he said. "Oh, hey …?"

Karen looked at him expectantly. He handed her the book – he couldn't make this mistake twice.

"Put this somewhere, huh?" he said.

She took the book from him and placed it on top of the beer fridge.

Satisfied, he hurried upstairs.

34.

Sherry lounged on Jake's bed, staring at the cracks in the ceiling. The damp of old towels, fast food wrappers, and Jake's aftershave permeated the loft – a bachelor's cocktail. The sheets were musty, too, and the mattress – now that she was just able to lay back and lounge – had a dip in the middle.

This was not home – the spaciousness of the king-size bed, with the mattress compiled from several layers of memory foam; the plush, duck-down pillows and cotton percale sheets; nor did it have the luxury marble tub in which she soaked so often to de-stress; there was nothing here but necessity coated in negligent housekeeping, and she was surprised to find that she was fine with that – for now, at least.

Footsteps thudded up the stairwell. Sherry propped herself into a half-sitting position on her elbows. Jake appeared with great theatricality, as if the sight of her overwhelmed and pleased him. It was goofy, but its spontaneity and novelty pleased her because it was that: this authentic thing with nothing else attached, no other context, no other focus but Jake being pleased to see her.

"Where you been?" she asked.

"Milo and I had some stuff to do."

"Skip's got a book signing, so I've got the day free."

She held out her hands. Jake took them.

"I want to apologize for the argument," Sherry said, "but I need to know I'm not just some fling. Or if I am," she paused as her voice caught in her throat, so she took a deep breath, "then you need to tell me."

Jake sat next to her. "I haven't had any long-term relationships. This is new to me so maybe I don't always handle it the best. But I *do* like seeing you."

"I was thinking of staying over," she said. "If that's okay."

The widening of Jake's eyes was fleeting but telling.

"That's a big step," he said.

Sherry bit back on her frustration. As much as she'd just been pleased, this was equally displeasing. The suggestion was for temporary accommodation. She could've told him that and defused the situation. But she didn't like his recoil. She saw herself as a convenience. There had to be more. She had to draw some commitment from him, even if it was tiny – anything but the status quo, because that just wasn't enough anymore.

"Where do you see your future?" she asked. "Not with me?"

"I ... don't think that far ahead."

"You must've thought that far ahead with the bar."

"True, but ..."

"Go on."

"I've worked in maybe fifty different bars. I remember them all. Some were long-term, some short-term, some just a one-off. I learned how bars worked, so I knew I could manage my own place. I've never had a committed relationship, so this is a big jump."

Sherry rose. "A woman needs to feel wanted. Not just for the sex. But in everything she has to offer. You're not ready for this – for a future."

She started away. It wasn't intended as bait. But he grabbed her arm and yanked her back. He might've been slingshotting her across the loft, but as out of control as she felt, then she was in his arms and he was rolling her on the bed. He kissed her, his hands warm and greedy. She did like this – nobody had ever wanted her this much – and she liked how giddy and tempestuous she could feel.

"Stay," he said.

She smiled.

"Or I'll tie you to the bed."

Sherry laughed as he kissed her again.

35.

Skip rocked on the recliner and sipped from his beer, watching as Tyson's tan Beamer turned into the drive, the headlights splashing across the veranda. He got out and waved in that breezy way he did everything, like he was acting in a commercial advertising good medicinal hemorrhoid relief. But then he stopped, his head titling this way and that, struggling to reconcile what he was seeing.

"Is that you, Skip?" Tyson said. "What on, or *off*, Earth happened to your hair?"

A shrill bark froze him halfway up the first step to the veranda. Skip dropped a hand and patted the ball of gray and white fluff nestled by the feet of his recliner.

"Is that your hair? Has it come to life?" Tyson said. "Or have you bought a dog?"

"I bought a *puppy*." Skip scooped the Siberian Husky onto his lap. "This is Silver."

Tyson, hands on hips, gawped. "And the hair?"

"I needed a change."

Tyson's eyes narrowed, honing in on some new detail. "Your face is sunburned."

"Tried to kill myself."

"*What?*"

"I tried to kill myself."

"With sunburn?"

"With the fake Xanax."

"Oh. *Oh!*"

"How long you been giving me those?"

"How long have I been getting them?"

It had been after the unexpected success of the first book, *Enraged*. Skip had struggled to deal with the sudden pressure to produce the follow-up and had asked Tyson to get him something that would relax him. Tyson had suggested marijuana. Skip had balked – the sweet, cloying smell gave him migraines. Tyson had then brought him a half-empty bottle of Xanax.

"Six-seven years?" Skip said.

"Then about six-seven years," Tyson said.

"They were never real?"

"The first bottle was – my doctor prescribed them to me after I struggled to deal with my break-up to Sherry."

"I'm sorry," Skip said – this was not something he'd ever known.

Tyson waved away the apology. "It was a tumultuous time – the break-up, business was struggling, and my mother had just died."

"You never told me—"

"Skip, I'm an agent. Our discourse is about you, *not* me."

It was strange to find Tyson had a personal life – one where he wasn't so glib and things *did* impact him. Skip wasn't sure why he should be surprised. If Tyson was a supporting character in a story, Skip would've nutted out a background to give him context. This reveal humanized Tyson; he could be vulnerable – and vulnerable enough that he'd required sedatives. But Skip never saw that. He only dealt with the shopfront.

"After that first bottle," Tyson said, "you started doing a lot of drinking, so I didn't think you'd notice if I brought placebos when you asked for more."

"Tyson, I'm appalled."

"Skip, my job's to take care of you. Not drug-peddle. So, I took care of you. It worked, didn't it?"

Skip didn't want to admit that the placebos had.

"Now let's go back to this suicide attempt – this is about Sherry?"

"We're done. I have a puppy now." Skip scratched Silver behind the ears, then set her down to explore the veranda. "That's unconditional love."

"This eerie calm worries me, Skip. It's not you."

"Swallowing all those placebos, waiting to die, was a cathartic experience."

Skip plucked a flash drive from his pocket and tossed it to Tyson. Tyson fumbled and juggled the drive, before it spilled through his hands and hit the veranda. Silver barked and tried to pounce. Tyson snatched it up. Silver looked up at him, as if expecting he might throw it and they could play again.

"What's this?" he asked.

"A collection of short stories I'd like to offer Gray's."

Tyson frowned. "*Instead* of the novel?"

"I'm still working on the book – I need an extension. But I'd like to release that, too."

"I'll suggest it to them – it could buy you some extra time. Are you sure you're okay?"

"I'm fine, Tyson." Skip got up. "In fact, give me a day or two, and I think I'll have something else for you."

"Something else? What?"

Skip smiled. "Just wait and see."

36.

The sound of a spatula scraping across a pan woke Jake. His eyes opened to slits; dust mites floated across fuzzy trails of sunlight punching through the window. Then it was Sherry's butt in the kitchen; she was naked except for a pristine blue apron – a pointed gift from Mom to highlight he should be cooking his own meals instead of relying on Milo (he would drop by regularly before The Rap), microwave meals, and fast food.

Jake hauled himself up into a sitting position.

Sherry neatly flipped a pancake. "Hey."

"What're you doing?"

Sherry lifted the pan and shook it – although her breasts and buttocks shook in a way that made Jake think of the way her body jiggled when he thrust into her. His erection stirred dutifully, almost as if it was trying to prod him out of his stupor.

"Pancakes," she said. "Hungry?"

"Sure."

Jake ambled into the bathroom, positioning himself above the toilet. He felt the pee ease from the bladder, but then he had to tense to stop himself. The toilet seat was down. No biggie. He lifted it and peed, although he became self-conscious of the urine hitting the water. He could picture Sherry out there listening to him. There was nothing abnormal about what he was doing – everybody urinated. But it was so common. So everyday. So non-sexual. He steered his cock so the stream of piss hit the basin.

Done, he flushed and span to face the sink. A red toothbrush and holiday-size tube of toothpaste sat on the counter, while a bottle of perfume and hair mousse occupied one of the shelves. Foreign bottles of shampoo and conditioner stood in the corner of the shower. He scoured the bathroom. What else had she brought? The tiniest unease crept in.

He went back out into the kitchenette and sat at the counter. Sherry served the pancakes, then sat opposite him. Jake smiled; it was her – sitting opposite him, mostly naked, playful, making breakfast. This could be something. The unease was nothing – trepidation about a new endeavor.

He shoved some pancakes into his mouth. "Delicious," he said.

"Thanks. I don't think I told you: I'm looking at a promotion at work."

"Promotion?"

She told him how the fiction publisher, Pria, had been earmarked as CEO, which meant her position would become open. Jake nodded, but his attention drifted as Sherry talked about overseeing fiction acquisitions, how she planned to market the authors, and an idea she had to push Luis Stauss (Jake had no idea who that was) commercially. Then she rambled on about revamping the office, which was much too sterile. Jake didn't retain a single word.

To compensate, he hugged her from behind as they deposited their plates in the sink and kissed her neck. She arched into him and stroked his cock. Now Jake found his equilibrium, and they had sex over the kitchen counter, against the fridge, and then on the bed. This was good. Great. As always. He saw her out when she went home – well, not home, because this was home now – to pick up more of her stuff.

Later, when Milo dropped in on his lunch break and they sat at the bar drinking beers, Jake relayed the discomfit he'd felt in the morning.

"I didn't know what to do," he said. "I didn't want her to feel like I wasn't listening, or I wasn't sympathetic, so …"

"So?"

"We had sex."

"I knew this was real!" Milo grinned. "And you know why I knew?"

Jake shrugged.

"Because you're very, very whipped, Jake."

"That's a cruel thing to say."

"Guys get whipped. We think we're hunters, but as you become more and more involved with a woman, you surrender all that authority. You don't even realize you're doing it. One day, she hollers at you to take out the garbage, and you're halfway out of the house before it clicks you're whipped. Just happened to you quick."

"She left her husband for me."

"Even *before* she left her husband, Jake. I could see the way you looked at her. It was really, um ... really ...?"

"Sweet?"

"No."

"Romantic?"

"No."

"Thoughtful?"

Milo clicked his fingers. "*Pathetic.*"

"Easy."

"Don't fret. That's the way it goes."

"You're exaggerating."

"Jake, you've given me *The Jake Rappaport Guide to Lovemaking: Search and Destroy*. You're all about reducing a woman to a quivering, wasted mess – like you're fighting mixed martial arts and have to score the submission, only your weapon is your cock and the orgasm the submission."

Jake wanted to tell him that was stupid, but it not only sounded right, but was arousing.

"There's a poetic irony that you've fallen this hard for her, that you're trying to find ways to please her in your Jakey ways. But commitment's scary. It scared me that I was going to be with this woman for the rest of my life, and I had to hit this standard every day, that I could no longer be irresponsible or stupid or unthinking and that I had to work toward building something."

"That doesn't sound so attractive."

"It's not a bad thing. Alice makes me want to be better than what I was when we'd hang out, drinking, trying to screw around."

"But don't you miss it?"

"Sometimes. When the house is a mess, the kids are screaming, Alice is hounding me about something, and it's like, *What've I gotten myself into?* But there are times I'm with Alice, or with the kids, where I'd never want anything else, and those regrets become just silly, immature quibbles. Trust me, this isn't a bad thing. It's not just personal growth. It's evolution. There's something better on the other side of it. You might not always think it, but it *is*. Embrace it."

Jake drank from his beer. Him and Sherry. Jake and Sherry. He pictured them waking up together every day – that wasn't so bad. Going to lunch at Mom's. That would be cringe-worthy, but they could joke about it on the drive home. He'd work The Rap. She'd be promoted. He wasn't so stupid that he didn't recognize the intellectual mismatch

– not that Sherry had ever flaunted that. But then he remembered how she'd droned at breakfast.

"What if she's not the right one?" he said, and was surprised to feel just the tiniest pang of dread that might be the case.

"Then move on. It's not rocket science, Jake. "

"I know, but …"

Milo slapped the bar and laughed. "You're worried about hurting her!"

"Well …" Jake didn't want to admit that was becoming a factor. "No, but, well …"

"Right!" Milo said. Then he laughed again. "Poor you, having to finally deal with somebody else's feelings. Imagine all those women who were developing feelings for you, or had hopes about being with you, only for you to fuck them and leave them."

"Okay, okay."

"It's almost karmic."

"No such thing."

"Uh huh. You know what it is? She's making you be real for her, and that scares you."

Real. Just the word Sherry had also used. Was this relationship vernacular? Jake didn't like it.

"It's not that …"

Milo gave him space. Jake was sure his silence, his inability to be glib and dismissive, condemned him.

"It *is* that," Milo said. "You're always projecting whatever image works best and getting out before they find out how shallow you are. Now you're being challenged, and you're scared. It's like the saying about the tail wagging the dog; all your life, your cock has been wagging you. Now *you* have to take the lead. Welcome to the world of relationships." He pulled his copy of *Cold Enterprise* from his pocket and waved it as he headed over to the door. "And give this a read – you'll like it!"

Then he was gone, leaving Jake with his insecurities.

37.

As Sherry got out of the car, she decided this wasn't the time for recriminations. It would happen. Skip would've stewed over this, built arguments (and scenarios) in his head, played them out obsessively, and prepared for every possible confrontation that could unfold. That had to be avoided. She'd take what she could and be gone. If there was to be any slanging, then Skip would learn that being a poor husband had consequences. That would rock his fragile self-image.

She heard a Mozart opera – she thought it might be "Lucio Silla" – wafting faintly from his study. It took her a moment to discern the rhythmic *clackety-clack* wasn't part of the music, but the sound of Skip's fingers racing across his laptop keyboard. Then she saw him sitting in his recliner on the veranda, laptop on his lap, a big unlit cigar in his mouth. Something shrill *yapped*. A little ball of fluff, along with the two of the most piercing blue eyes in a mask of silver, charged to the top of the steps and barked. The typing stopped. Sherry paused at the foot of the veranda. The Husky wagged its tail.

"You shaved your head?" Sherry said.

"I needed a change."

"And you bought a dog!"

"A *puppy*," Skip said.

The Husky snarled at her.

"The cigars?" Sherry asked.

"Mmmm, I'm still getting the taste of them – I don't know if they'll stay."

"The chair?" Sherry's voice grew shrill.

"This is a lot of questions."

Sherry took a deep breath, and as she let it out imagined all the tension seep from her body. "I came to get some stuff. Let's not make this any harder than it has to be."

"It's not hard at all."

Sherry didn't like how calm he was being. Or assured. This was not Skip. He was a manchild - well, usually. Now he was just ... what? *Enigmatic.* He'd become a character in one of his books - purposeful, focused, and composed.

She put her foot on the bottom step.

The Husky barked.

"Can you get control of your dog?" Sherry said.

"Puppy."

"Whatever he is —"

"*She.*"

" —can you get control of him ... her?

"Silver!" Skip said. "*Silver!*"

Silver continued to bark, leaving Skip no choice but to pick her up. Silver whimpered and licked at his face. Sherry started up the steps. Skip opened the door and ushered her in. Sherry sniffed as she passed him - surely, he had to be drinking, but all she smelled was boiled milk.

She charged up the stairs but juddered to a halt in the bedroom doorway: her luggage and travel bags were already out, as well as several big cardboard boxes. The closet was open - Skip's clothes hung in one half, while the other half was now empty.

Sherry knelt by one of her suitcases and opened it. Her clothes had been carefully folded and packed. She went through the rest of the luggage and bags – everything had been perfectly filed away: informal wear in one case, formal wear in another, delicates in a bag. He'd been meticulous. The cardboard boxes held personal items – her jewelry, pictures, books, and various little knickknacks she'd picked up over the years.

Her legs grew unsteady as she rose. She'd wanted to make a stately exit, for him to listen as she shoved her things into bags. He'd robbed her of that. He didn't even want to try and hold on. It was petty to want that, but she did. Tyson had pleaded. He'd been pathetic. But not Skip. Skip was apathetic. This was not at all what she'd expected. But perhaps Pria was right – he was a savant with little understanding of societal interaction.

She grabbed a case filled with casual wear, lugged it down the stairs, and banged open the front door. Skip was rolling a ball down the length of the veranda for Silver to chase. Sherry dropped the case so it thumped onto the veranda. Skip spun; Silver jumped and looked at her quizzically.

"You packed my things," she said.

"Just clothes and possessions. You chose the furniture, paintings, decorations, and all that stuff. When you get settled, we can sort that – and the house – out."

"It's all this easy for you."

"No. It's not easy. But you were a status symbol for me. That's not your fault. That's mine, thinking I needed somebody as brilliant and beautiful as you to complete me, to appreciate me. I don't know what I was to you."

Sherry prepared to fire a salvo but had nothing to offer. Skip had entranced her with his creativity, and she had believed that would spill over into the other areas that had mattered. She thought he'd live life the way he wrote it – passionately and grandly. But she'd fooled herself. That's what relationship misfires were: self-delusion that a coupling could work. This had just been a longer self-delusion. Like Pria had told her – a façade. It was strange that Pria had foreseen all this; Sherry had expected an entirely different narrative.

"You don't, do you?" Skip said.

And here was Skip being so philosophical. He was in his writing. His prose suggested he was confident, insightful, and enlightened, a writer who keenly understood the intricacies of relationships, exploited their vulnerabilities, and offered denouements that few would consider. But that wisdom and maturity had never spilled into his everyday life – until now. Here was some semblance of a man she'd thought he'd be, but which was only beginning to revealing itself. How could he have taken so long to grow up?

"What's happened to you?" she asked.

"When you read a book, the outcome's *always* the same. We're all stories, moving to an inevitable outcome – until we become self-aware. Then you get control of the narrative."

"And how did you become self-aware?"

"It doesn't matter. We're not bad people, Sherry. Well, mostly. You're not. I'm selfish and myopic, but I've become comfortable in that. You deserve much better than me. However, having said that, you're cheating on me – that's *you*, isn't it?"

Sherry couldn't answer. Because it *was* true. That *was* her narrative.

"I'll send somebody for the rest of my stuff," she said.

On the drive back to The Rap, she mulled over Skip's sudden insight. Sherry could see she was capricious, constantly chasing something new, enjoying the initial glamour because it was exciting, but once that dimmed, she would begin looking elsewhere.

She had always wanted constancy in her life. Professionally, she'd accomplished that – she was respected in the industry, and now that hard work would pay off with a promotion into Pria's role. But personally, she had unwittingly practiced a whimsy that was, upon reflection, embarrassing. *And* immature.

She had to change.

38.

Wet from a shower, hair dripping all over the floor, Jake paced around his loft, a towel wrapped around his waist and his phone jammed between his ear and shoulder.

"Mom, I think you'll like Sherry—"

"Who is she?" Mom asked.

"Somebody I met—"

"Somebody who? When do *I* meet her?"

"Mom, it's—"

"Is she one of your whores?"

Jake bit back on the anger. It never worked with Mom. She would just condemn him for the way he was speaking to her. Dad used to argue with her but, realizing the futility, had learned to become a sponge that absorbed her vitriol. At times like this, Jake had no idea how Dad did it although, in all likelihood, he had just been so passive that he'd found solace in drinking, even knowing it was killing him. Maybe that had been the point.

"Well?" Mom said.

"Mom, she's not—"

"You've been hiding her from me."

"I haven't—"

"You're going to live together – is she moving in with you?"

"Yes—"

"That loft is hardly a place for a relationship."

"It's only temp—"

"Doesn't she have her own place? You said she's a professional woman. Where's she been living?"

Jake's heartbeat accelerated until he fleetingly feared he was having a heart attack – just like Dad. But this was only the dread Mom elicited. Jake couldn't tell Mom that Sherry was married, that she was leaving her husband, that their relationship had begun as an affair. That would give Mom inexhaustible material for disapproval and castigation.

"Her lease is up," he said. "So she's moving out until …"

Silence. Jake could almost hear Mom exploring the possibilities in her head – until *what* exactly? And Jake didn't know how to expand upon his answer. Until what? Until he and Sherry found a place together? Until her divorce? Until whatever came next. Buying The Rap was a big decision, but it had involved nobody else. Milo was right. This was no longer just about him.

"You're going to live together," Mom resumed, "yet you've been keeping this relationship from me. I want to meet her, Jake."

Jake pictured Mom and Sherry sitting at the kitchen table at Mom's. Mom would fire questions, like a catapult battering away at a castle's walls. How would Sherry handle it? Probably fine – she was self-assured enough to not to be flustered. If anything, Sherry would weather Mom's assaults and impress her – a professional classy woman. Almost on cue, he heard her bounding up the stairs.

"Mom, I've gotta go," Jake said.

"Jake, we need to talk—"

"Sure – we'll work out lunch or something."

"Jake—?"

"See'ya, Mom."

The moment he'd hung up, Sherry shot through the door, both her hands locked into the handle of a big suitcase. She eased it down delicately, as if whatever it contained was fragile, then planted her fists into her hips and sighed.

"Skip already had everything packed," she said. "Can you get the rest? I want him to see who I'm with. I know it's petty, but right now petty seems *right*."

Tension arced from Jake's neck and into his shoulder blades. Sherry's hands slid into the towel and onto his buttocks. This would be good – he'd grab Sherry's stuff and face this prick down. It'd be fun – like the book signing, but without the pretense. Jake's towel dislodged and slid down his legs.

"Well, well, well," Sherry said.

When he fucked her on the bed, her legs splayed high and wide above her own shoulders, it was with that same intent to break her, to see her yield to him. But she fucked him the way she always did – her hips bucking, her fingers clawing into his shoulders, as if she wanted to show him she could take everything he gave her, and give it right back

In his experiences with her, one of them would always relent. But now, something new happened: he thrust harder, the collision of his hips into her crotch and thighs a rapid drumroll throughout his loft. Her body bounced, and her cries elongated into a long wail. But she rode him until they were moving in concert. The attempted domination crumbled. Now she matched his rhythm, until Jake reveled in a union of body and mind. They were one. He'd heard stories from Milo and had always thought them sappy and cliché. But now he was a part of this beautiful woman. They were sharing this. She was giving him every bit the pleasure he was giving her. It lasted just seconds, and then he was coming uncontrollably, coming like he'd never known before, coming until his crotch throbbed and his legs spasmed. He collapsed on top of her, his breathing labored. Her arms came around his back as if she was shielding him from the world. She patted his head. He kissed her.

"That was great," she panted in his ear.

He didn't have the energy to respond.

But by the time Milo picked him up later – in a Toyota Tacoma that Milo had borrowed from a workmate – Jake was feeling decidedly upbeat. This was the beginning of something new. *Special*. Jake looked forward to coming home to Sherry. She'd be grateful. They'd have celebration sex.

"You're okay with her moving in now?" Milo asked.

"Yeah. I am."

"Good for you, man."

Milo's GPS guided them to Skip's address – a double-story house with big windows that a cleaner probably washed, and beautiful gardens that a gardener probably tended. Skip would have servants – people to come in and do all the housework while he sat in his study, typing away, nerding it out on his next cunting bestseller.

Once Milo had reversed into the drive and they'd gotten out of the car, Jake saw Skip seated in a recliner on the veranda. Music drifted out from the house – classical of some sort. The only thing that Jake had gotten right was that Skip *was* typing away. A Husky puppy ran to the foot of the steps and yapped at them. The typing stopped.

Skip put his laptop on the floor and rose from his recliner. He glanced at Jake with surprise, if not apprehension, and then grinned at Milo, overplaying a welcome that was nothing but forced.

"If it ain't my best friend!"

Jake was sure he detected a tremor in Skip's voice – he was trying to be glib, trying to play it cool, but he was nervous about this encounter. His gaze fleetingly took Jake in again, then averted with the dread of somebody who didn't want to make eye contact. He was scared. Good. Great. The fuckwit wasn't going to smart-mouth his way through this.

"Hey!" Milo grinned. "You remembered me. Cool."

"Read *Cold Enterprise*?"

"Just about finished. Your best yet."

Jake coughed as interjections raced through his head: *I'm here for Sherry's things!* Or, *We're not here to be friends.* Or, *Listen, cunt, I don't want any trouble – I came for Sherry's things.* And Skip would shuffle and defer and step aside. As they walked past him, Jake would quip something like, *She's the greatest fuck – not that you'd know*, or, *She's got the tightest little butt*, or, best yet, *We laugh about you after we fuck* (even if it wasn't true).

Skip pointed at him. "Congratulations on your relationship."

Jake smelled Skip's fear. He was trying to bluff. Nerds and fuckwits did that.

"I gather you haven't started reading my book."

Now Jake was taken aback. It was such a random thing to say. Not a single rejoinder occurred immediately to him, and the few that came belatedly were lame: *Nerds read; I've got better things to do; I've been too busy fucking your wife* – the latter was puerile, but it would do. Only Skip was already mowing ahead – a little too quickly, but he was pushing on nonetheless.

"She want the furniture and all that stuff?" he asked. "She did all the decorating."

"Just her things," Jake tried to snarl.

Skip scooped up the Husky and swung open the screen door. "Straight up the stairs, second door on the left."

"You working on something new?" Milo asked.

Jake shoved Milo through the open door. Milo's head span this way and that and he whistled appreciatively at the opulence – crystal vases that sat on pedestals, abstract paintings, and a furry rug that covered the landing. Skip had said Sherry had decorated. This was her. These were her tastes.

And they were familiar in a way that elicited a trepidation Jake had felt just like that moment he'd learned Dad had died, and what had come next, what had muscled through the overwhelming grief and punctured the all-encompassing sadness was the realization that from this point on, he would be dealing with Mom alone.

Mom.

Being here was like being in Mom's place.

39.

Skip stacked the drinks bucket with bottles of Budweiser. He was doing okay with this. At least that was what he told himself while the panic frittered in his mind until he was sure it would shred his composure. This was like high school – this was like seeing himself exposed for what he was: frightened, nervous, and jittery. He could attempt to bluff as much as he liked, but Jake brought it all back.

Stripped of the façade and the affectation, taken away from the keyboard and art of the storytelling, Skip faced the prospect he was nothing but that same stupid kid psychologically anorexic on things people took for granted, like socializing, interacting, and relationship building.

Packing ice into the bucket, he made his way back out to the veranda, and saw Tyson, hands on hips, frowning at the Tacoma in the drive. Silver wagged her tail, pleased to renew an acquaintance. Tyson drifted up to the veranda and absently scratched her head.

"Company?" he said.

"Just the guy Sherry left me for and one of his friends."

Tyson blinked. "Come again?"

"Guy Sherry left me—"

"Skip, I don't swear often, but what the fuck?"

"They've come to pick up Sherry's stuff." Skip thrust the bucket in Tyson's direction. "Drink?"

The screen door opened, and Jake and Milo emerged, both with a case in each hand. Tyson gawked at them.

"Tyson, Jake, Tyson, my best friend Milo, Milo, Jake, my agent Tyson Valance."

Milo dropped his cases and offered his hand. Tyson took it more as a reflex than anything. They exchanged pleasantries like they might've been old high school friends who'd bumped into one another on the street. Tyson, now in cruise mode, aimed his open hand at Jake. Jake kept holding his cases in a way that made his shoulders and biceps swell to their fullest.

Skip offered the bucket around, glad it weighted down his hands to stop them from shaking. "Drink?"

"Sure!" Milo reached for a beer.

"Milo!" Jake said.

Sighing, Milo picked up the cases and led Tyson back to the Tacoma. Skip watched as they shunted the cases into the back. Sherry would hate that – she prized her luggage. Jake would have to explain why it was scuffed or, worse, dented.

"Skip, have you lost your mind?" Tyson asked.

"I don't know if I ever had it."

Jake and Milo returned – Milo pausing, like he wanted to ingratiate himself into the conversation, but Jake poked him so he kept moving. The two went into the house. Skip was glad Jake wanted to be brusque about this – they wouldn't be here long at this pace.

"Your life's come apart," Tyson said, "your wife's left you, you've bought a dog—"

"Puppy."

"—you've cut your hair, and the man Sherry's fucking is gallivanting in your house like he was doing no more than-than-than—"

"I'm writing."

"Skip!" Tyson threw his arms up dramatically. "*Skip!*" Now his hands covered his face but, after several moments, he spread his fingers so he could peek out. "Skip, tell me ... what are you writing exactly?"

"A screenplay."

"A screenplay?"

"*Cold Enterprise*. I thought of a way to adapt it."

"You thought of a way to adapt it?"

"How about we pitch a limited series instead?"

"A limited series instead?"

"Tyson, you're repeating me."

"I'm sorry – I'm stunned."

"It just came out. Also, got some short stories I could smack right into that anthology."

The screen door opened, and Milo propped himself there, big cardboard box held out in front of him.

"Did I just hear you say that you're writing short stories?" he asked.

"Yeah," Skip said. "I want to do an anthology."

"Sounds great."

"You want to read them?"

"What? You're kidding? Really?"

"I need an alpha reader."

"*Me?*"

The screen door jutted open, and Jake eased himself out, a cardboard box cradled in each arm. He glared at Milo but walked on down the veranda and to the Tacoma. Milo rolled his eyes with great theatricality.

"I better get back to it," he said.

"Give me a day or two on those stories and I'll print them out. You know your way here now."

Milo grinned. "Cool!" He followed Jake down the drive.

"Skip, you can't be giving your work out to the public," Tyson said. "That's how plagiarism suits begin."

Skip sat in his recliner, set his bucket down, and opened a Bud. He lifted Silver onto his lap. Silver flipped onto her back and offered her belly. Skip scratched her until her eyes squeezed shut and her ears reared back. Well, here was something – some*body* – who'd love him despite his frailties.

"Skip!" Tyson said. "Are you taking any of this seriously?"

He leaned against the veranda's balustrade and folded his arms across his chest. Skip had never seen him so indignant. It was because of Sherry. Tyson expected him to fight for Sherry just as he had. Tyson expected him to be devastated. Tyson expected him to be human. He couldn't understand the indifference.

"I think that's the problem," Skip said.

"What is?"

"I've been taking all this too seriously – me especially."

"Skip, you're the most frivolous man I know!"

"Externally, but internally ..." Skip tapped his temple. "It's hard being me, Tyson. It's hard pretending to be anything close to normal."

Jake and Milo continued to make junkets. On the final trip, Jake emerged with one last box, brow glistening, and panting. He started down the steps, then stopped, and scowled at Skip. Milo paused, empty-handed and wary.

"You wouldn't believe," Jake said, "how we fuck."

Skip flinched – even Tyson and Milo did. Jake's smile was cocky. For a disconcerting moment, Skip was disoriented. This *was* like school – the way the popular kids would insult him, laud their seeming superiority over him, and how they'd revel in humiliating him.

"I believe it," he said. "I've seen pictures."

Jake took half a step up onto the veranda. Skip instinctively retreated back into his recliner, sure this was going to turn ugly – no, not turn ugly, but Jake was going to make it ugly. It made no sense, though – Jake *had* Sherry. Skip had been wronged. Jake had no moral ground to justify his anger.

If Jake had been one of Skip's characters, Skip would've explored *why* he would behave this way, and the only answer was because Jake had nothing else. He had to keep asserting what he believed was his superiority because if he didn't, he had to face who he truly was – just some adulterer who had nothing of any value in his life.

And all this over Sherry – over a relationship. Skip thought about how he'd tried to take his own life, how he had floated in the pool, awaiting death. He hadn't been scared. If anything, he'd been whimsical. There'd been no fear, and the fear now seemed stupid – redundant. All because of this dick who didn't deserve to elicit such a response.

Milo lifted an arm to make sure Jake progressed no further up the stairs. Even Tyson took a precautionary step forward in case he needed to intercede – a gesture that surprised Skip, and which he appreciated, given Tyson was about the least physically confrontational person anybody could meet.

Skip set Silver down, and rose from his recliner. He knew this had to be done – he had to face down the bully. But it wasn't just Jake, but everybody Jake represented – all the people who'd picked on Skip, who'd derided him, the whole miserable fucking past.

Slowly, Skip offered his hand for a handshake.

Uncertainty flickered across Jake's face – this wasn't the way things were meant to go. Jake had won Sherry, and he was meant to rub that victory in Skip's face. This was not the narrative Jake expected; it was something so new he couldn't reconcile it, and grew almost petulant in his surliness.

"Fuck you," he said, then hurried down to the Tacoma.

Milo backpedaled slowly. "Sorry about that," he said. "You serious about those stories?"

"Yeah, sure."

Milo pointed at him. "I'm gonna take you up on that, you know?"

"Cool."

"See'ya!"

"Bring beer!" Skip said.

"Buds?"

"I'm mixing it up nowadays – surprise me!"

Milo waved a hand in acknowledgment.

They got into the car and reversed from the drive. Once they'd pulled out from the house and driven down the street, Tyson's arms finally uncrossed.

"That was tense," Tyson said.

"It was an experience," Skip said.

Tyson's perennially smooth forehead tried to crease. "An experience?"

"You're overreacting."

"One of us has to!"

"You still love her, don't you?"

"What? That's outrageous!"

"You're jealous."

"I'm nothing of the sort!"

"It's fine," Skip said. He sat down, and scooped up Silver again. "Sherry's smart, beautiful, and mesmerizing. But I was with her for the wrong reasons. I think you were, too, but you're probably still lamenting what you think it might've been. I bet you still fantasize about being with her. Miss Sherry Valance – well, she didn't even take my name. And why would she? We're the hangers-on. We're the nobodies."

Tyson's lips drew thin.

"She wasn't right for you, Tyson."

The anger blushed through Tyson's bronzed complexion. "I've never been so insulted in my life," he said. "You can consider our relationship terminated." He started down the steps.

"Our personal relationship or our professional relationship?"

Tyson stopped halfway down the drive and pivoted on one heel. "How dare you be so glib! Our personal relationship, of course!" He spun back. "And email me your screenplay!"

He stormed over to his Beamer, parked on the curb. If Skip had written this scene, the engine would roar to be commensurate with the driver's displeasure but, instead, it turned over just as it would've any other time Tyson started the car, and the Beamer coasted down the street.

Skip scratched Silver behind the ears.

"He'll be back," he said.

40.

Relax.

That's what Sherry told herself, as she lounged back in a hot bath. Any other time, she would've been able to unwind. But the tub was cramped; even with her head nestled on the porcelain rim, the water barely covered her breasts, her shoulders sticking up and feeling the cold. She couldn't fully extend her legs – she had to plant one foot against the end of the tub, her knee poking up out of the water like the head of the Loch Ness monster; the heel of her other foot rested on the opposite curve of the rim.

Her phone, sitting on the corner of the bathroom sink, vibrated, then rang. She considered leaving it, but then realized it might be Jake – it could be something about getting her stuff from Skip. But once she sat up and grabbed the phone, she saw it wasn't Jake at all, but Pria.

"Pria," she said.

"Hello, Sherry," Pria said, her voice clear and bright, "how are you? How goes your relationship malaise?"

Sherry's hand tightened around her phone. "Have you heard something?"

"No, of course not – I called with news. Has something happened?"

Sherry lounged back in the tub.

"Sherry?"

"I've left Skip."

"What?"

"It wasn't working."

"And this other man—?"

"I've moved in—"

"*Already?*"

"Temporarily. Well, probably."

"Sherry, this is drastically impulsive," Pria said, as if forcing the words over sandpaper. "Even for you. Are you sure you're doing the right thing?"

"What I know is that being with Skip *isn't* the right thing."

Silence. Then the clink of glass and something being poured. Water? Gin? Both? Pria had never struggled for words. She had seduced authors, swayed editorial meetings, and – time and time again – convinced superiors of who they should pursue and at what cost, and who they should cut loose. She hadn't always been right – nobody ever was in publishing. But she was always rousing and eloquent.

"Pria?" Sherry said.

Pria let out a deep breath. "It's your decision, Sherry. And I know your life must be tumultuous right now, but I'm afraid I have bad news. You've been overlooked for my position."

Sherry sat up in the tub.

"It's just that they feel with the upheaval, we should be pursuing somebody external who can come in with a fresh perspective. I'm sorry."

"Thank you for calling me," Sherry said, rising out of the tub.

"It's the least I can do."

After Sherry had hung up and as she was getting dressed, the incongruities in Pria's call poked through, like the issues in an underdeveloped plot of a first draft novel. Pria had been upbeat when she'd first called. Would she be upbeat with bad news? Her manner had changed after hearing about Skip. Had Gray's truly overlooked her for Pria's job? Would they? Doubtful, unless Pria – the new CEO – recommended against it. And why would she?

Sherry picked up her phone, started to drag up Pria's number, then decided another call would not do. This had to be done in person. Sherry had to see Pria's face, had to put her in a position where there was no retreat.

She sprung down the stairs two at a time, and almost sprinted to the parking lot. The drive into the city bordered on reckless, Sherry charging through amber lights, and weaving through traffic until her Saab skidded into Gray's underground parking and screeched into two spots.

The elevator was torturously slow, although its uninterrupted ascent reminded Sherry that everybody should have gone home for the day. *Should* have. But Pria would be working. Of course, she would be. So, when the doors slid open, Sherry charged across the eighteenth floor, grabbed the knob to Pria's door, and only paused when she heard the mix of squealing and heavy breathing.

She swung open the door.

Sherry's mind refused to reconcile the sight: Pria's back was to Sherry; Pria, in just a shirt, seemed perched on the edge of her recliner, facing the backrest, her legs jutted up until they were perpendicular; her elbows teetered on the edge of her desk for balance; she breathed deeply and rhythmically, as she would for yoga.

The top of a head popped up above Pria's right shoulder – the flushed face of Ben, the intern. "Oh!" he cried

And now Sherry could make sense of it: Pria was straddled upon Ben's lap in the throes of sex.

Pria glanced over her shoulder, and then threw her head back and gasped. "Sherry!"

Sherry placed her hands on her hips, feeling suddenly maternal, like she'd walked in on her son masturbating.

Pria sighed, gracefully disentangled herself from Ben – even in her position, she was graceful – and slid from his lap. Her legs were lithe and toned, and she had an angled little tattoo of an ankh to the right of a small, neat, but inverted triangle of pubic hair. She fetched her skirt and buttoned it around her waist, as if she'd been interrupted baking and was just refastening her apron. Ben, naked, rocked back and forth on the chair, his hands clutched over his crotch, not knowing what he should do.

"Did I not get *your* job because I left Skip?" Sherry said.

"My dear," Pria said, as she took out her flask of gin and poured them each a double shot, "I tried to warn you."

Ben continued to rock.

"Dear, please leave us," Pria told him.

Ben scrambled for his clothes, flew around the table, and shot out the door.

"And you're fucking an intern," Sherry said. "An intern! It's a cliché in itself!"

"I told you I had a secret to keeping young and vigorous," Pria said, holding out a glass of gin. "Sex is it. You've learned that yourself, haven't you? With this new man? My husband and I are open." She snorted. "A monogamous marriage in today's age. It's like leaving a child in a chocolate store and telling them they can have as much chocolate as they like, but of only one type."

"Then why didn't I get your job?" Sherry finally took the gin from Pria.

"Discretion, Sherry. I warned you. I *warned* you. You are the most measured, deliberate editor

I know, yet impetuous in your own personal life. I implored you to be patient and yet, here we are: you've left Skip and moved in with this man. You're always chasing the thrill that comes with a new relationship. Do you not see that?"

"This is about my peace of mind."

"Sometimes we need to temporarily sacrifice peace of mind to advance in life. You're an excellent editor – truly, the most gifted editor I have ever mentored. But you are *just* an editor. Skip's about to become a six-figure author. We can't afford to antagonize him."

Sherry lifted her glass of gin to her mouth, tightened her hand around it, then hurled it into the wall. The glass shattered, spraying the wall in gin and the floor in fragments. Pria was unmoved. She sipped from her own gin.

"Speaking of clichés," she said.

"I have other options, you know."

"Have you? This *could* be scandalous. Most publishers would shy away from any negative publicity. You could stay here in your current role, but I imagine you now consider that untenable. I did hear that Oliver Townsend from Palette approached you at Skip's launch. They're small. Edgy. Perhaps they'll take the risk. It would be several rather gargantuan steps backward, though – financially, professionally, and in reputation.

But you might enjoy the challenge of editing new authors and building such a small fiction list into something substantial."

Pria could've handled this in so many different ways; she could've discreetly warned Sherry how leaving Skip would impact her professionally. Even if it had cost Sherry the promotion, she would've respected the honesty and considered staying.

Instead, Pria had chosen to disassociate herself from any possible splash back once people heard – and the industry *did* gossip. It would be like a high school locker room. Now Sherry had to face that alone – well, she had to face it with Jake. She was curious how he'd respond, but inexplicably felt he'd be okay. He was now her only ally.

She and Pria were done – not least of all because of Pria's staggering sanctimony and hypocrisy. She was fucking an intern! It would've been so easy to leverage that information to extort the role of fiction publisher. But then what? Pria had chosen a course that had irreparably damaged their relationship.

"Consider that," Sherry gestured at the splatter of gin on the wall, "my resignation."

"I'm sorry, Sherry. It's politics. You understand, I'm sure."

Sherry stormed from the office.

41.

"What the fuck was that?" Milo said on the drive back to The Rap. "Again, you gotta be like some teenage bully! It's like you haven't grown up at all!"

Milo's recriminations went on and on and on and on, devolving into the sort of lecture he must've used on his kids when they misbehaved. He was condemning, he was eloquent, he was persuasive, and yet not a single word sunk into Jake's head because the shock was impenetrable.

"Are you listening to me?" Milo said. "Are you?"

Jake couldn't get the comparisons out of his head: Sherry's place looked like Mom's place. And Sherry's place looked like Mom's because *they* were similar – they weren't common women. They weren't tawdry. Jake had thought of Sherry as *classy*. Maybe she was, but in a way that was aristocratic. *Uppity*. Mom had that down, too.

"Jake!" Milo said.

"I've got a question to ask you. And I need you to be honest."

"What?" Milo's tone was sullen.

Jake took a deep breath. "Am I fucking my mom?"

Milo laughed and spluttered at the same time. "*What?*"

"Sherry's house – it's like my mom's, right?"

Milo was stoic for several moments. Then he grinned. "Shit!" He laughed. "Shit! Shit! *Shit!* This makes a lot of sense now."

"What makes a lot of sense?"

"The way you treat women – fuck them, break them, leave them. It's like an Oedipus complex."

"An edible what?"

"Not edible. Oedipus – a sexual desire for the parent – but you're doing it vicariously through all these women. Your mother dominates you. You get back at her through sex with all these women. You dominate and break her over and over and—"

"Okay! But Sherry …?"

"Is she really like your mom?"

Jake tried to find dissimilarities, but they were few. Both were strong, independent, and dominant. Mom was controlling, too, though. Sherry wasn't – at least not yet. Jake tried to hold onto that. But it wasn't entirely true. Sherry *had* been controlling about commitment. She'd driven the pace and the seriousness of the relationship – maybe she wasn't doing it consciously, and it definitely wasn't malicious, but it had been in a way that had discomfited Jake.

"Or is this like you're scared and trying to find a way out?" Milo asked.

Could it be that simple? Jake couldn't puzzle it out. He *wanted* that to be the case, but it was a hollow belief.

After they'd returned to The Rap and unloaded Sherry's stuff, they stood back and surveyed it all. Her bags and boxes carpeted the floor. She'd smothered him out of existence, which was what Mom had done to Dad. For as long as Jake could remember, Dad had never had a single footprint in the house.

"You okay?" Milo said.

"I don't know."

"I had a panic attack the night before I married Alice – all I could see was being trapped in this relationship forever."

"And now?"

"And now I'm happy I'm trapped in this relationship forever. Ease up, Jake. Maybe you're just looking for an out. New *is* scary, but that doesn't mean it's bad. Take the plunge."

Once Milo was gone, Jake dashed into the bathroom and doubled over the toilet. Nausea flooded through him until his legs grew weak and trembled. His breath shortened until the bathroom span. Surely he couldn't be *this* afraid of commitment, could he?

"Jake?" – Sherry, from the loft.

He staggered from the bathroom. She was sitting on the bed, hands folded in her lap, face downcast.

"What's … wrong?" he asked.

"I didn't get the promotion."

"What?"

"Fiction publisher," Sherry said. "With Skip and me splitting up, they don't want to antagonize him, so they passed me over. I resigned. I need a drink. Something strong. Scotch?"

"I'll get some," Jake said.

He darted down into the bar, grabbed a bottle of Johnny Walker Black Label and two glasses. Alcohol would help. It would relax him. It would probably even help him think clearly. He was too anxious. He *needed* to relax. Once he relaxed, he could put this in perspective.

But after Sherry had downed a couple of scotches, she said, "We should look at getting a place together." She waved her arm to encompass her things. "This is going to be too small."

Jake opened his mouth as the anxiety reignited. He did like her. Well, he did like fucking her. She was great to fuck. They fucked awesomely. But he'd always known that. The query was what lay beyond that. Could it be this thing Milo had said, this complex thingy? Or was it a proper relationship? Was the commitment the thing that terrified him?

They kept drinking until a new parallel flashed into Jake's mind: he'd become Dad. Dad had drunk to cope with Mom. Why hadn't he left her? Had he ever tried? He must've contemplated it. Or did he drink to stay in it? To make it bearable? Mom had been an attractive woman when she was younger. Jake shuddered. Now it was going back to that newfound territory he didn't want to face, let alone explore.

"You know what I need now?" Sherry said, pushing him down.

"No, wait ..." Jake said.

She kissed him. "This is a good thing," she said. "I need to change my life. Especially with men. I keep getting involved with the same types – you're different."

"How?"

She nimbly unbuckled and unzipped his pants. "Simple. Uncomplicated. In a good way. In the *best* way."

Her touch repulsed him. All he saw was Mom. And yet his erection stirred – a traitor to his reservations. She doused him in scotch, went down on him, and rode him as he lay limp under her. He kept seeing Mom's face, heard her castigations. Sherry bent over him, kissed him; he thought of kissing Mom on the forehead, of her sticky make-up, and then grew angry. This couldn't be about her. It was about Sherry. It had to be.

He rolled her, took her with a mindless ferocity, entreated every trick and secret he'd learned about fucking, but she met his every assault, countered him adeptly and found his susceptibilities, until he was coming when he didn't want to, and his face sunk into the pillow above her shoulder, panting.

"That was intense," she breathed into his ear.

He flipped onto his back; she rolled with him, cuddling into him. She was hot and sweaty and her chest heaved, and as disheveled as she was in her afterglow, she was triumphant and fused to him so he couldn't get out of bed. Milo might've called it love, but Jake felt it now, felt it truly, felt it honestly that Sherry was Mom's avatar, and every coupling with her was his attempt to pulverize her in a way he'd never done with a woman, and in a way he'd never been able to one-up Mom.

"You okay?" Sherry asked.

He couldn't tell her. She'd invested so much in him. She'd invested *everything*, and that invited the well of guilt that Freckles had tapped. This was not him. It was never him. And yet it was *now*, and he didn't know how to reconcile this duality.

"Big day," he said. "Just tired."
"How was Skip?"
"Flippant."
"That's him."
"I tried to ..."
"What?"
Jake was unsure if he'd upset her.
"Well?"
"I sorta bullied him."
Sherry laughed, then ran a hand over his chest. "Why?"
"I don't know – just because it was him."
Propping herself up on one elbow, she kissed him on the temple – kissed him approvingly, the way Mom would when he was a kid and he'd done something good.
"I appreciate the gesture," Sherry said, "but I disapprove of the behavior. Skip's not a bad guy. He's just ... *juvenile*."
They drank late into the night and finished the scotch. Jake wanted to find oblivion but found only Sherry. She fellated him to life. He tried to find his way out by fucking again, and reviled himself, that this was his only recourse. He turned Sherry around and took her from behind, but then an irrational fear crept in: he couldn't see Sherry's face, but if she could, if she turned to look at him, it wouldn't be Sherry but Mom.

Horrifyingly, he came just as the thought took form, and as he flopped onto his back, he tried to divorce himself from it, tried to enforce a separation between it and his ejaculation. Just a coincidence. That was it. He didn't come because he'd thought of Mom. It was just a coincidence.

Sherry kissed him, then burrowed into him, like she was a ship planting anchor. Jake loosely curled an arm around her, but more to pronounce the physical dissimilarity to Mom. Sherry was soft and relaxed and soon asleep, but the restlessness that pulsed through his limbs drove him to carefully untangle himself from under her and get out of bed.

He went down into The Rap and opened a fresh bottle. For a moment, for just the instant, he found some peacefulness standing here in the middle of his dream. He'd neglected the bar the whole day. No doubt Karen or Luke had locked up. But this was meant to be his future – and his life.

His gaze fell on the drawer under the bar. He pulled open the top drawer; both sets of Sherry's underwear were nestled there.

This was exclusively their connection: fucking. The few times they'd talked about other things – like her work – he'd disconnected. So that left the fucking. And now that was tainted. All that remained was the woman who lay in his bed.

Her keys sat on the counter behind the bar. Grabbing them, he unlocked The Rap, and went out to the rear parking lot. Sherry's Saab was the only car there. He let the cool night air wash over his naked body and drank from the scotch.

Fuck it.

He was sure he'd be pulled over, or he'd run the car into a telephone pole, or he'd get lost, and he wished for any of those alternatives, but it wasn't long before he was driving up the winding road to Skip's house, then pulling into the drive. The lights in the house were off. Jake checked the time on the dashboard: 1.47am. He gulped from the scotch.

Stumbling out of the car, he followed the headlights up to the house. Wind rustled through trees, crickets chirped, and something *clack-clacked*. He downed what he could of the scotch, then lifted the bottle above his head. Even as muddled as his thoughts were, he pictured the route he'd taken to get Sherry's bags from the bedroom, which meant the bedroom window was top right. He cocked his arm back.

"I wouldn't do that."

Jake froze. A dark blur rose behind a dim glow – a computer laptop – on the veranda's balustrade and took a step forward. Jake lowered the bottle and advanced warily until he could make out Skip, eerie in the beams of the headlights, his shadow projected dauntingly large on the wall of the house behind him.

"I was going to throw it onto the roof," Jake said. "Get your attention."

"Here I am – attention gotten." Skip smirked. "Didn't have time to dress?"

"Fuck you."

"Well, you seem to be going through the family. Read my book yet?"

"What?"

"My book – the one you had at the book signing. Have you read it yet?"

Jake snorted. The audacity of the man – this is where his focus went? On whether Jake had read his book? It was such an unlikely question. But then, maybe that's all that mattered to this fuckwit: his own ego, and the people who stroked it for him.

"No, for fuck's sake," Jake said. "I haven't read your fucking book."

"Didn't think so. If you had, I think you would've gleaned at least one truth from it."

"I'm not looking for any truth."

"Then why you're here? You're looking for something, right?"

Cornered. So easily, too. And yet as much as Jake was looking for something, he wasn't sure *what* exactly. Understanding of some sort, most likely. This relationship hadn't gone like any of Jake's other affairs: guilt-ridden women; partners trying to reclaim them; fuck-buddy ecosystems that he could depart. And there it was: it began with a simple question.

"Why didn't you fight, man?" Jake asked.

Skip sat on the balustrade, surveying Jake from head to toe. "I thought you'd be bigger."

Again, surprise. None of this conversation was going the way Jake expected.

"I'm plenty big," he said.

"Okay."

"And I know how to use it."

"Good on you."

"I do." Jake took another drink from the scotch.

"I believe you."

"Good."

"Sherry know you're here?"

Jake shook his head.

"You come here and want to keep playing the tough guy, huh? You want to fight?"

The challenge startled Jake.

"Want to take a shot at me?" Skip asked.

"What?"

"Want to take a shot at me? Bet a guy like you monstered the geeks like me in high school."

"Too right."

Skip leaned over the balustrade, until his face hung above Jake's. Jake's hand tightened around the neck of the scotch bottle. Skip closed his eyes. Jake lifted the bottle. It would be so easy to club Skip; Jake could kill him, although a beating was more appropriate – something the twit could remember him by. But that felt woefully inadequate right now.

The last two times they'd interacted, Jake had been able to sense, to smell, and *see* Skip's fear, his nervousness, his diffidence. But something had happened. This Skip was unafraid. *Tranquil.* Like he'd elevated, *evolved*, above it all, and that worried Jake more than anything. Sherry wanted to change. Skip had changed. As for himself?

He lowered the bottle.

Skip's left eye opened, then the right. He straightened. "You know what, Jake? You know what the reality is? You know why I didn't fight for Sherry?"

"Why?"

Skip took a cigar from his pocket and popped it in his mouth. "You smoke?"

"No."

"A new vice – probably another affectation." Skip took a Zippo from his pocket, lit it up and puffed the cigar to life. "I had girlfriends in high school, Jake. Frumpy girlfriends. Nerdy girlfriends. I had one Sherry-type, and she ditched me because it was uncool to be with me. And that was it. Cool guys like you got the Sherry-types. That was the way of things – that's the shit thing about being a teenager: there *is* a way of things, a social order, a coolness hierarchy." He blew out a smoke ring. "And now I have a beautiful wife, she ultimately chose a cool guy over me. Again. Life's a cycle." He grimaced. "So, you've gotta learn, or you stay in that fucker until you're so dizzy you never get your orientation back. You asked me why I didn't fight for my wife?"

Jake guzzled down some scotch.

"It wasn't my place to fight for her, Jake. I had to fight for myself."

"And you're happy? Even if you're alone forever?"

"Then I'll be alone for the right reasons."

Jake let the scotch bottle slip from his hand and clunk onto the grass.

"Sherry fought for herself. What about you? You come here looking for … what? An out? That's not my responsibility. You did this. You want me to save you from yourself?" Skip laughed. "That it? You cowardly little motherfucker. That is it, isn't it? At the end of the day, what're you left with but yourself? You can't face that, can you?"

He was right. Jake saw it now and cringed. He was transferring responsibility. That's where his anger had repeatedly come from. He'd expected Sherry to re-dedicate herself to Skip, or for Skip to fight for her – just like husbands had always fought for the wives he'd seduced. Then Jake could walk away, possibly not in good conscience, but *good enough*. He wanted an out that he didn't have the courage to create himself.

He had trapped himself in this – physically, he couldn't surrender Sherry; emotionally, he could never commit; intellectually … he didn't know how intellect factored into any relationship. Maybe that was the problem with relationships but likelier it was – he conceded begrudgingly – the problem with him.

"Did you ever love her?" he asked.

"Very much. And she loved me the same. Looking back, I'm unsure it was for the right reasons, which is maybe why we grew apart and didn't know it. That's not what a relationship should be about. And not with her. She wants to please whoever she's with – well, at least until she feels that's unreciprocated. She deserves that. And I am what I am: *selfish*. You've done us both a favor, Jake. Thanks."

Skip offered his hand.

And yet another surprise. This had never happened – no man had ever thanked him for fucking their partner, for damaging their relationship, for wrecking their marriage. Yet here was this fuckwit, this ... Jake didn't even know what Skip was. He was unclassifiable. And he came offering a handshake – *again*.

He might as well have been holding a gun.

Jake heard Mom's voice ring in his head: *We have to talk about this.*

He stumbled back and fell on his backside. Scrambling to his feet, he lurched for the car.

"Hey!" Skip said. "Come back! You shouldn't be driving!"

Jake leaped into the car and started the engine. He expected Skip would charge down the drive, but the headlights lit him up exactly where he had been on the veranda, puffing away on his cigar. Jake reversed the car onto the street, and saw the shadow on the wall of the house behind Skip move, like a reaper coming to claim him. Jake hit the accelerator until the tires screeched, and drove home, rehearsing the break-up.

He parked out back, let himself into The Rap, then trudged up the stairs. Light spilled from the door. He slowed the higher he got, until he slipped into the bedroom. Sherry sat on the end of the bed, a silk pink robe draped around her. She jumped up. Some of her cases and boxes had been stacked on other cases and boxes to form an aisle from the door to the bed.

To her.

This was it. He was just going to have to tell her.

"Jake!" she said. "Where've you been? I've been worried sick!"

Concern.

Concern!

Concern hadn't been something he'd expected. But of course, she'd be concerned. He'd snuck out. Naked. Taken her car. Drunk. She would've been worried. Naturally. Because she cared about him. She wasn't just about herself. She'd sacrificed herself for him. Like when they had sex. She gave herself to him, to whatever he wanted. Because she wanted to please him. To make him happy. Like Skip said. She wasn't combative – not the way Jake explained sex to Milo. She was giving. And he took. And took. And took because he thought it granted him superiority; he thought he could pervert her and take pleasure from it; he *did* want to break her, just as he had every other woman, but here was one who'd proved unbreakable, and whom he couldn't escape.

"Jake?"

Sherry took a step forward. Her leg poked from the slit of her robe. He wanted to untie the robe and throw her onto the bed – or at least his cock wanted him to do that. It wanted him to take her concern and warp it into lust until she wailed in his ear. And yet she repulsed him. Not her, because she was gorgeous. But the Mom connotation. The motivation behind every woman he'd ever fucked, their collective hurt, mystification, and incredulity, blossomed, until it became an emotional nuke.

"Jake?" Sherry opened her arms. "Talk to me!"

Jake looked down at his crotch. His cock – proudly growing erect before his very eyes – was a goddamned troublemaker and a liar and a fiend. It still wanted him to take up the battle once more, to destroy her just like he'd done with every other fuck he'd had, to notch up another Freudian victory over Mom. But this was a war he couldn't win. This was a war that was going to kill him.

"Stop ignoring me!"

That was Sherry. *Sherry*. Sherry! He had to tell himself that over and over because in his drunken confusion, he could imagine his cock demanding the exact same thing from him: *Stop ignoring me!*

He opened his mouth. Here it came. Here came the break-up speech.

"Jake!" Sherry said. "We need to talk about this!"

Jake's head snapped up. Every word he had been about to speak died an inglorious death on his tongue. Drunken realizations eddied in his mind, concreted, and weighed him down with the dawning horror that he was incapable of honesty, of sincerity, and he was nothing more than this ugly little manbeast.

And that was it.

Absolutely nothing else remained – nothing but this yawning emptiness he couldn't fill, the acknowledgment that he was too cowardly to make meaningful change, and the self-loathing born from all the women he'd lied to, used, and discarded.

"Jake ...?"

He ran to Sherry. She opened her arms wider.

"Jake ...!"

He leaped past her, bounced on the bed, and dove through the window.

"*Jake!*"

Glass shattered around him.

The cold night embraced him.

And the ground welcomed him with all its unforgivingness.

42.

Skip twirled in his chair before his laptop, the cursor blinking mid-word, as if it was puffed and in need of rest.

His phone vibrated, and then the opening guitar from Blue Oyster's Cult "Don't Fear the Reaper" sounded. He'd programmed the song for just one caller. Muting the stereo (currently blaring Mozart's opera "Idomeneo"), he grabbed the phone and headed into the kitchen, Silver pouncing at his heels.

"*Hello, Tyson,*" he wanted to say, but all he got out was "Hell—"

"Brilliant, Skip!" Tyson said. "Just brilliant! If I may say, it's better than the novel! Inspired! Amazing! Astonishing! Marvelous! Flawless! Can you believe that? It *is* without flaw!"

Skip took a moment to process two streams of thought: the first, that there were no Buds left in the fridge; and the second, that he wasn't sure where Tyson's praise was directed.

"The short story anthology or the—"

"The screenplay, Skip! The adaptation to *Cold Enterprise!* It's insanely good. Insanely. You've nailed it. Revolutionized it! This is spectacular."

"Tyson, calm down – nothing's that good."

"This is, Skip. This *is*! But I always knew you had it in you. Gray's have also given you another twelve weeks for the novel. With Sherry's departure—"

"Sherry's departure?"

"You didn't hear?"

"No."

"From what I gathered, they wanted to groom her for Pria's position as fiction publisher once Pria became CEO. But after you two split up, Pria was worried how that would affect you if you were answerable to Sherry, so passed her over."

The sudden disorientation that hit Skip took seconds to process. He could live without Sherry the partner. He didn't know if he could live without Sherry the editor. The inter-office politics weren't something he was usually privy to (and something both Tyson and Sherry had shielded him from), but he loathed that he'd been used to qualify Gray's decision.

"That's not fair," he said. "She's the best editor I've ever had. *Ever*. You tell Pria—"

"It's done, Skip. Sherry's gone over to Palette – remember Palette? You met their CEO, Oliver, at your launch. He recruited Sherry to head their fiction division. Luis is following her. Gray's released him from his contract when he kicked up a storm. They're in short-term upheaval, but they'll settle. They're too big not to. And maybe this is good for both of you. New start and all. It's definitely good for Palette."

It was one of the few times Skip didn't feel Tyson was being facetious. Maybe this was the course to take – as painful as it might be for now. He'd relied on Sherry personally and professionally. Maybe it was time he grew up and truly took responsibility for himself.

"You okay, Skip?"

A knock on the front door echoed down the hall. Silver spun and barked. Skip trawled out from the kitchen. It would probably be the cops again, asking about Jake, about his state of mind that night, about why if he was so drunk, Skip didn't try harder to stop him from getting behind the wheel, like a damned road accident had killed him or something.

"Yeah," he said.

"I'll let you get back to the writing!"

"Tyson?"

"Yes?"

"Thanks," Skip said.

Silence. Their relationship had always been specious – although through no fault of Tyson's. When he spoke, his voice warbled.

"You're welcome, Skip," he said. "Any time."

Skip hung up, shoved the phone in his pocket and opened the door. He grinned. Silver wagged her tail. It wasn't the cops, but Milo, carrying the printout of his anthology in one hand and a six-pack of Two Birds in the other.

"Beer?" he said.

43.

Sherry trundled down the hospital corridor, can of Coke in her hand. She took a deep breath when she arrived at Jake's room, then entered.

Jake's eyes nervously flitted away. Most of his body – including his head – was encased in plaster, with only his right hand free. His mother stood at his bedside, her left hand under the bedsheet and positioned above his crotch. Sherry heard it now: Jake's stream of piss filling a bottle. Mom arched her brows.

"The one thing he doesn't break," she said.

Mom took the bottle and went off into the adjacent bathroom. Jake's gaze pivoted back to Sherry. She forced a smile as they listened to Mom empty the bottle, flush the toilet, and use the sink. Then she was moving with a deliberation that belied her age. She slipped the bottle into its holder on the side of the bed and reached across to take the Coke from Sherry.

"Thank you, dear," she said. She opened the can, stuck a straw in it, and pressed the top end of the straw to Jake's mouth.

Sherry sat in one of the bedside chairs and rested her hand on his left arm. Skip had been unpredictable, and he had a frivolous and self-destructive side, so Jake's simplicity had been assuring. But, obviously, that simplicity had a filter easily overloaded.

His face contorted until he was grimacing in pain, and then he mumbled something indecipherable. Everything was indecipherable now – as far as communication went, he relied on scrawling into a notepad with his good right hand, But he only ever had one demand.

Sherry picked up the morphine clicker from the bedside. "You want this?"

His head moved minutely back and forth.

Sherry placed the clicker under the fingers of his hand. "I don't know what got into you," she said. "Diving out the window."

"It's the drinking," Mom said. "This lifestyle he's led. Bars, whores, and more bars. Is it any wonder he unravels?"

"The drinking will kill us," Sherry said. *If it hasn't already.*

"You listen to her, Jake. She's right. You have so much of your father in you. *Too* much. The drinking killed him, you know? A heart attack – yes, a heart attack after all that drinking had destroyed his health. Sometimes, I think he meant to drink himself to death. And you know why? Because he was *weak*."

Jake's response was a series of mumbles.

"You're fortunate you have us," Mom said. "Although you'll be the death of me." She slumped into her chair. "Maybe the counselor can make sense of what's going on in your head."

"A hospital counselor." Sherry rolled her eyes. "He needs a psychologist. Or a psychiatrist."

"A team of psychiatrists," Mom said. "Or you can talk to me. You know that, don't you? You can always talk to me. Don't be like your father, stewing over everything. Talk."

Jake gestured to the bedside cabinet, where several books were stacked. Mom eased herself up from her chair and grabbed them.

"You want one of these?"

Sherry got up. "I need to get to work."

"Now?" Mom said. "You just got back."

"New job. I need to make a good impression."

"Do you see that, Jake? That's dedication. That's commitment and responsibility. If only that was something you understood."

"I'll see you both ..."

Sherry kissed Jake – or kissed Jake's plaster – on the top of his head, then let herself out of the room. Immediately, the air grew clearer. *Lighter.* It wasn't so much Jake's mom, and nor was it Jake's condition. If Sherry could be certain she loved him, she'd stay by his side. But now all she saw whenever she looked at him was his diffidence, and his lack of purpose.

The drive to Palette reinvigorated her. Unlike Gray's ostentatious office high-rise, Palette's was located in a loft just outside the city, nestled among the trees, the parks, and the sense of something so idyllic that it might've been some serene pocket that existed outside the rest of the world. As she cantered up the zigzagging stairwell, she plunged into its homeliness. Somewhere, she'd lost this intimacy with the creative aspect of publishing. It had become business during her time at Gray's, and while that remained a stark reality, she was reminded that storytelling was a deeply intimate medium.

The top floor was spacious with a scattering of tables – Palette employed only a handful of designers, editors, and the single publicist. Framed blown-up book covers adorned one wall, framed reviews another, and a dining setting by an enormous fish tank filled with colorful fish lined a third. Oliver's unpartitioned office was in the top corner.

Sherry took a chair opposite him. He was reading Luis's novel in hardcopy – they'd acquired it from Gray's when Luis had indicated he would do no promotion for the book, and nor would he re-sign with them following the book's release. They'd been reluctant initially, until Sherry had hinted it would be a shame if the public learned about Pria's fling with an intern. Pria had been aghast. Sherry had told her it was karma. They'd released Luis.

"This is a beautiful book," Oliver said. "What's Luis like?"

"He's not a beautiful man."

Oliver laughed – he was always ready with a laugh. "We need to take him out to dinner," he said. "That'd be a great thing to do as a group."

His eyes twinkled in a way that suggested that was something he'd also love to do just with her, although he would never be inappropriate. She'd learned Oliver had a high moral standard.

But this was where it would be so easy for her. She could ask him out for a coffee. They'd talk. She'd engage with him. The rest wrote itself, as it had with Jake, and Skip, and Tyson, and every relationship she'd had. Pria had nailed it. The need to be wanted had dictated her life and provided only short-term gratification. At some point, she had to get it right.

She could pursue this, or just let it hang unspoken between them.

Opening her mouth, she was sure for the first time in her life that what she was going to say would be the truest she'd ever been to herself.

44.

Pain throbbed through Jake's body. He was sure if it always returned to the same place, he could brace himself. But sometimes it flared in one leg, then exploded in the other, then pulsed in his lower back, then rippled through his neck, then burned in his face, then cramped in his left arm. And the morphine wasn't doing much good, as they'd begun to regulate it.

"So, what shall we read?" Mom asked.

She fanned the books on his bedside cabinet, exposing the bright, ebullient cover of *Cold Enterprise*. Jake's face tensed. How'd that get here? Sherry? Had it been a joke? Likelier it had been Mom, who'd obliviously gathered some things from the bar and the loft. The fingers of his right hand wriggled and extended, trying to grab it. He wanted to hurl it through the window.

"This one?" Mom said, misinterpreting his agitation.

She put the books back on the bedside cabinet, sat down, and opened *Cold Enterprise* to the title page.

"Oh," she said. "This is signed – to *you*. 'You can cheat me, and you can cheat yourself … but only for a time. Ultimately, there's always a reckoning – right, J–J–Jake? It doesn't get any more complicated than that. All the best. Skip'. Hmmm. What does that mean, Jake?" Her face grew hard. "We need to talk about this."

Jake clicked for the morphine but knew it wouldn't kill the pain.

Acknowledgments

Thank you to my Novel class way back in 2008, who workshopped scenes from the story: Sally Muirden, Therese Mobayad, Lucas Reidy, Tess Evans, Blaise van Hecke, then later, Alistair Ong, Louise Le Nay, and Laura Bovey, among others.

Also a thank you to my writing group: Beau Hillier, Blaise, and Gina Boothroyd, and another thank you to Blaise van Hecke, who read multiple drafts of the finished story, saw various incarnations, and provided feedback, encouragement, and listened to my self-doubt.

Thanks to Kim Lock, who's such an invaluable writing confidante and advisor.

Thanks to talented young designer, Rosie Giuliano, for the fantastic cover image!

Finally, thank you to Ryan O'Neill, for his insight and feedback.

Writing's a tough gig, so it's always helpful whenever you find anybody who believes in what you're doing and helps you get there.

Thank you.

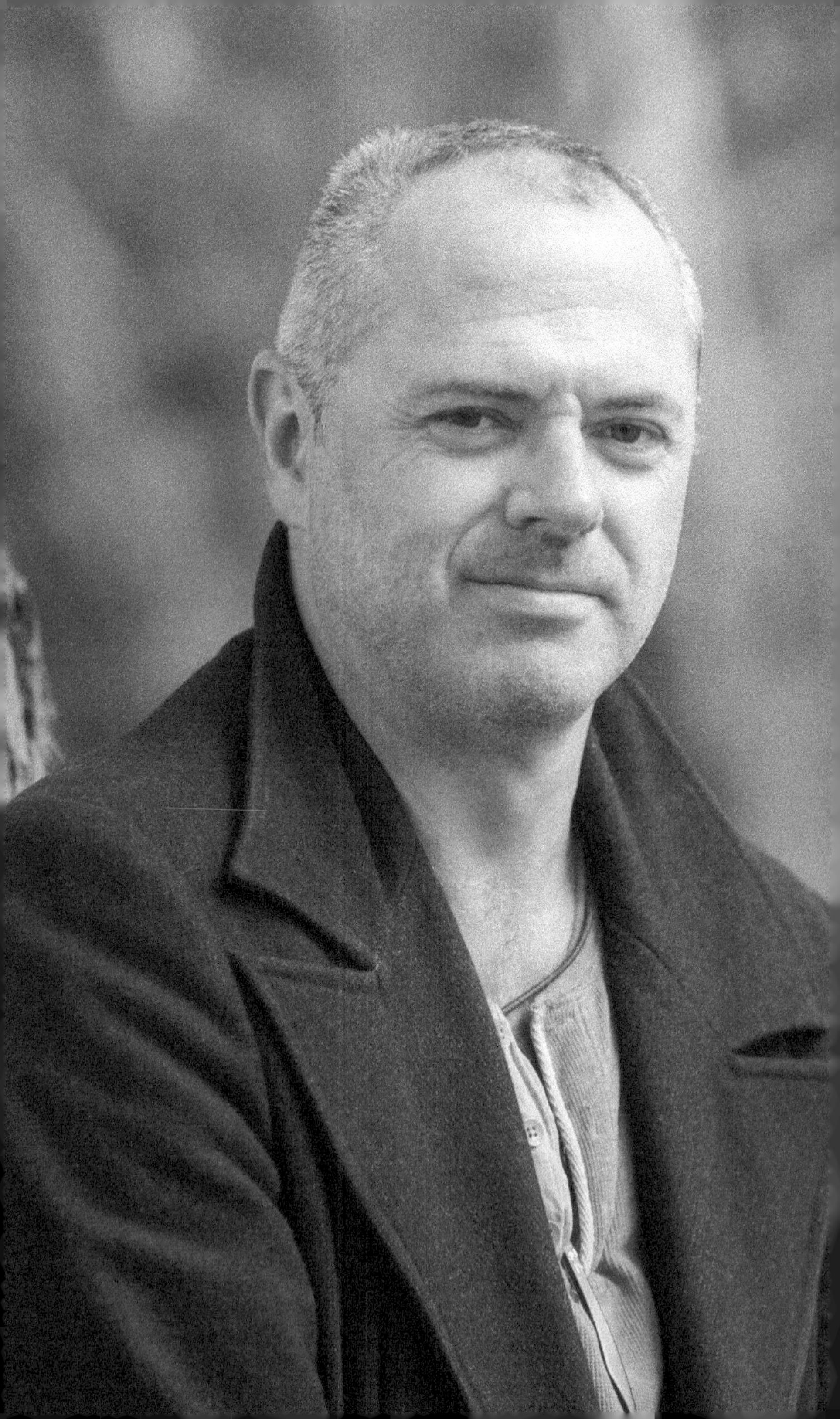

About the Author

Les Zig has wanted to be a storyteller since he was a kid reading *The Lord of the Rings*.

He faced mental health challenges as a teen, and then recurringly as an adult, and grew fascinated with human behavior, the way people interacted, and how everybody defines themselves individually, as opposed to socially.

Humor is a constant through his writing, just as it is in life. Even during our darkest times, absurd moments present themselves.

When he's not writing, he's thinking about writing, and has also written articles, blogs, and screenplays.

You can find out more about him at his website:

www.leszig.com

PRUDENCE
A Tempestuous Night of Pervasive Desires

LES ZIG

A prestigious nightclub.

An aging hostess battling to retain her marquee.

A beautiful and enigmatic woman with unparalleled ambition.

A noble widower searching for love.

Two irreverent barflies
who may not be what they seem.

Three couples whose relationships will be tested until they question everything they know.

A jaded stripper trying to find her self-respect.

A modest twenty-something man gambling on a shortcut to fortune.

And a mysterious old man who will reach into their hearts and twist and pervert everything they hold dear.

Over the course of one night, temptation, seduction, and rage will touch each of them.

And their lives will never be the same.

Prudence is a dark psychosexual thriller that explores human boundaries, the desires they define, and the secret acts that shatter them.

The Slush Pile Demolitionist

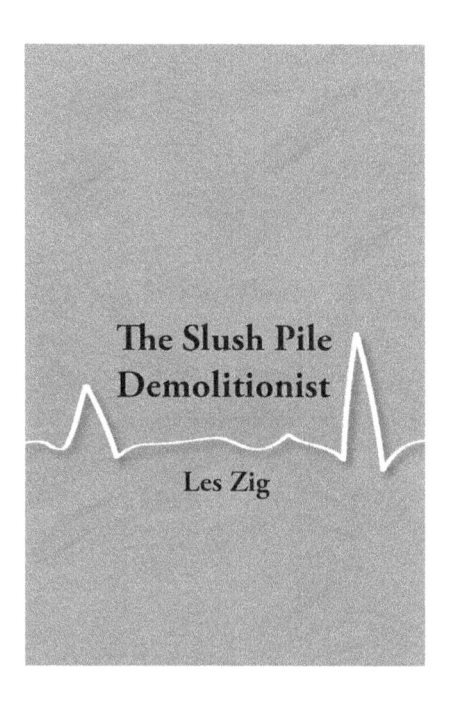

Les Zig

A mature-aged student undertaking work placement at a boutique publisher learns there's more to writing than talent, and that success demands its own toll.

When a multinational publisher looks for somebody to fill the vacancy heading their fiction department, a spited senior editor is determined to win the position at any cost.

A middle-aged writer struggling with a lack of success, years of rejection, and questioning his own self-worth, re-examines just why he writes, and whether to go on.

The Slush Pile Demolitionist features three short stories centered around writing and publishing that explore the darker side of creativity, the desperation of insecurity, and the uncertainty of the future.

Other novels by Les Zig ...

Pantera Press
August Falling
Just Another Week in Suburbia

ECG Press
Prudence

As Lazaros Zigomanis ...

MidnightSun Publishing
This

ECG Press
Song of the Curlew
The Shadow in the Wind

Busybird Publishing
Pride

Printed in the USA
CPSIA information can be obtained
at www.ICGtesting.com
LVHW041330051124
795764LV00002B/96

9 780645 485394